THE TROUBLE WITH DIGGING TOO DEEP

DIANE KELLY

D1738630

Cover design by Taylor Dawn, Sweet 15 Designs

❀ Created with Vellum

ACKNOWLEDGMENTS

Acknowledgments: Many thanks to Cecilia Conneely and Tracy Hartman for proofreading and providing feedback on my draft of this story. You ladies rock! A big thanks also to my fellow Trouble in Tumbleweed series authors – Melissa Bourbon, Christie Craig, and Lawrence Kelter – for being so great to work with. It's been fun getting into trouble with y'all.

TEASER

Teaser - CPA Debra Ott finds herself suddenly single after catching her dentist husband "drilling" a patient. Good thing she's too busy with her audit of Tumbleweed Pawn & Pistols to dwell on her heartbreak. When an elusive gun supplier fails to confirm his account, Deb has to dig for answers. But the more she digs, the more danger comes her way. Could digging too deep mean she's digging her own grave?

CHAPTER 1
DRILL BITS

WHOEVER SAID you can't have it all was right, but sometimes you're lucky enough to get damn close.

I have a job that I love, running my own accounting practice in downtown Tumbleweed, Texas—Debra Ott, CPA. Most people call me Deb, but my fellow number nerds call me "Debit," as in debit and credit. I have a wonderful daughter, Hayleigh, who married an equally wonderful young man last year. The two recently purchased a cute starter home in the T-weed suburbs last year. Maybe I'll be a grandmother soon! I also have an affectionate-when-he-feels-like-it orange tabby named Buddha because of his ample pussycat paunch. And last, but certainly not least, I have a successful husband with a thriving dental practice. Like any marriage, ours has experienced its shares of ups and downs. But lately, things seemed to be on an upswing and Allen had been treating me like a queen. I figured I'd reciprocate this morning by surprising him at his office with his favorite dark roast coffee from the Cowboy Coffee Shop.

I stepped into the coffee shop and took my place in line. The place bustled, as always. The steamer sputtered, patrons chatted, spoons and forks clinked. The enticing aroma of roasting beans filled the air, and I took a deep breath to drink it in. Norman, the surly barista, slung drinks with a practiced efficiency and perpetual frown. The guy had all the charm of a mafia mob boss, which, if rumor was right, he'd actually been in a former life. Norman was stocky with salt-and-pepper hair and, despite being in his sixties, wore a teenager's wardrobe of T-shirts printed with sarcastic phrases. Today's read *No hablo stupid*.

Mikenna, the thirtyish manager of the coffee shop, was the yin to Norman's yang. She had an energetic perkiness that matched the coffee she percolated, greeting everyone with a smile and a "good morning!" Her golden blonde ponytail bounced as she flounced around behind the counter, serving the drinks, taking payments, making change, spreading caffeine and cheer.

As the mochas and lattes left the counter, the line slowly progressed. I inched my way past the pictures of classic cowboys that hung on the wall. John Wayne. Johnny Cash. Gene Autry. Will Rogers. Directly in front of me stood Reverend Roach, a skinny scarecrow of a man with dark hair. While I tried to save the Tumbleweed residents on their taxes, he tried to save their souls. He'd been after mine for years. Luckily for me, he was tied up with another soul at the moment, that of our town's mayor.

Mayor Waylon Spurr was a direct descendant of Tumbleweed's founder, who had run a mercantile and rented the rooms above it—along with the flesh of beautiful young women. Mayor Spurr insisted there was no truth to the spurious stories about his ancestor being a pimp, but the tales passed down from earlier generations said otherwise. The mayor's cheap toupee sat on his head, looking like something that had been snaked out of a drain in the shower of a men's locker room. I wasn't sure what was worse, the fake hair sitting atop his head or the fuzzy, mold-like hair growing out of his ears and his caterpillar eyebrows.

When the Mayor stepped up to the counter, Reverend Roach turned to see who was behind him. Fortunately, a colleague turned away from the counter with her coffee and caught my eye before he could tell me, for the millionth time, that he'd missed seeing me in church last Sunday. *Maybe if your sermons didn't wander aimlessly for what felt like forty years.* If nothing else, he made his congregants sympathize for the Israelites.

"Deb!" called Kathleen, who worked as manager at the local bank. "How've you been?"

"Insanely busy," I said. "Thank goodness April fifteenth is behind us now." We'd passed the tax deadline last week. I'd spent the entire subsequent weekend in bed, catching up on sleep and my favorite sitcoms.

"The Stocktons applied for a big loan from the bank," she said. "Half a million, I believe. Said they're gonna expand the Pawn and Pistols. Are you performing the audit?"

"I am. They want to move quick, too, but don't you worry. I'll make sure their financials are in good order."

She waved a dismissive hand. "Don't kill yourself working late. The audit is just a formality required by the underwriters. I can't imagine the Pawn and Pistols will be turned down. That place has been in business since the dinosaurs died out here."

The Permian Basin was an enormous oil field thanks to the dead dinosaurs who eventually transformed from overgrown geckos into fossil fuels. It was odd to think that our cars ran on tyrannosaurus juice. But it was true that the pawn shop had been in business forever. Warren Stockton's grandfather had established the store in the early 1900's and passed it on to his offspring when he died. Warren's father had run the place for years before turning it over to his son.

With a "let's do lunch soon," Kathleen headed on her way.

Reverend Roach finished placing his order and, finally, it was my turn at the counter. I ordered the dark roast for Allen, and got myself my usual skinny vanilla latte with coconut milk. *Yum!* I handed Mikenna some cash for the coffee and dropped a couple of dollars plus my change in the tip jar. "I'm taking the coffee to go. Mind putting them in a carrier?"

"No problem." Mikenna slid the two cups into a sturdy carboard carrier to make them easier for me to transport, and held them out to me.

I took the drinks and thanked the young woman. "Have a good day, Mikenna. You, too, Norman."

He merely grumbled in reply, not bothering to turn around from the espresso machine. I fought a chuckle. Thank goodness my husband was pleasant to be around. In fact, he'd been especially so recently. I'm not sure what had gotten into him, but he had a fresh spring in his step. Must be those new vitamins I'd bought for him. They were designed especially for men over fifty.

Carrier in hand, I left Cowboy Coffee. The late spring day was bright but bearably warm. Another month and the sun would beat down on us relentlessly, punishing us for daring to live in the remote, unforgivable desert of west Texas. But, despite the heat and dust storms, the place had a certain charm.

I headed past the pawn shop, the theater, and the police station, before turning down a side street. I strode over to the next block. My husband's dental office was on the first floor of a two-story medical building, sandwiched between an ophthalmologist and a pediatrician. A man held the main door open for me, and I stepped into the lobby. I headed down the hall, using my elbow to push the lever on the dental office door.

Inside, three patients thumbed through magazines as they waited to be called to the back for their appointments. Lynette, my husband's receptionist, smiled when she saw me come in. "Hey there, Deb."

I raised the cup carrier. "Thought I'd surprise Allen."

She angled her head to indicate the hallway behind her. "He's in room three doing a consult on veneers."

I headed back to room three. The door was closed. I raised my hand to knock—patient privacy and all that—when I heard strange sounds coming from the other side of the door. There was an *ooh*, an *ahh*, a grunt, another grunt, and then my husband's voice crying, "I'm coming!" *Why the man felt like he had to announce every orgasm I'll never know.*

I opened the door, patient privacy be damned. My husband and a redhead were going at it in the reclining chair. Allen's back was to me, his pants bunched around his knees, the hem of his white lab coat flapping up and down to reveal his bare ass as he thrust his pelvis. Like a good patient, the woman beneath him had her mouth wide open to emit an *aaaah*. She gasped in pleasure. My husband was drilling her all right, but he was filling the wrong cavity.

The two had been too involved in their lovemaking to hear me come in, and maintained their momentum as I walked over to the chair, turned the bright spotlight on them, and called out, "Surprise!"

Allen yelped and twisted to look behind him, but there was no room on the narrow chair. He rolled off the other side, inadvertently slamming his elbow into the table of sterilized instruments and sending it crashing to the floor. He landed on his butt on the tile, his eyes wide. "Deb!" He scrambled to his feet and pulled up his pants. "It's not what it looks like!"

It was bad enough he'd cheated on me, but to treat me like an idiot was more than I was willing to take. It hurt to realize that spring in my husband's step hadn't come from the vitamins. It had come from banging this woman. She looked familiar. I peered at her, and recognition slapped me in the face. *She's the interior decorator we'd hired to redesign our kitchen!* The thought that I had trusted this woman with something as personal as my home infuriated me further. But the house I'd shared with Allen wouldn't be my home any longer. No way could I live in a place that reminded me of him, of this disgusting scene. It was ironic that I'd just been thinking how he'd treated me like a queen. Then again, I supposed he had treated me as well as Henry VIII had treated most of his queens.

"Surprise!" I called. "I brought your favorite coffee. Enjoy!" I pulled his cup from the carrier, thumbed the lid off, and tossed the drink onto the two of them, wishing I'd walked faster on the way over. The coffee had cooled enough that they wouldn't be scalded. *Damn.* At least it would leave a nice stain on his lab coat.

Leaving my husband and his mistress dripping and sputtering in my wake, I left the dental office without a backward glance and stalked back to the square.

Tookie, an older woman who ran the diner on the square, knelt in front of the chalkboard sign outside of her eatery. She wrote on the board, no doubt listing the specials and the pie of the day. Tookie's Diner served the world's best pies. She bought many of them from a Tumbleweed transplant named Cassie who baked freelance. Cassie worked magic with flour, vanilla, and a rolling pin. We always ordered one or two for the holidays. Birthdays, too. Tookie eyed me as I approached. "What's put a burr in your britches, Deb?"

"Is it that obvious?" I asked, stopping and looking down at her.

She narrowed her eyes. "Your aura's blood red. But even if I couldn't read auras, that scowl on your face was a big clue."

I exhaled sharply. "I just caught my bastard of a husband with one of his patients. They were—" *Fucking? Doing the nasty? Bumping uglies? Banging?* Though I was fifty myself now, I'd always been taught to respect my elders. So, trying not to be crude, I went with "—in flagrante delicto."

"Flagrante delicto?" Tookie cocked her head. "Is that the new Mexican place on the other side of the river? I heard they make a mean margarita."

"No," I said. "It means I caught them—"

Tookie waved a slightly-gnarled-with-age, dismissive hand. "I know what it means, hon. I was just making a joke. You look like you could use a laugh."

"A laugh," I agreed, "or a double-barreled shotgun." I mimed raising a long gun in front of me and taking aim. "I'd blast my husband in the ass like he deserves."

Tookie chuckled. "I'd like a front-row ticket to that show. That man's been a damn fool." She reached up a hand. "Mind helping an old lady stand up?"

I took her hand and helped her leverage herself to a stand.

On her feet now, she tucked the chalk into a pocket on her apron. "Wait here a minute. I've got something that will cheer you up."

As she stepped into her diner, I glanced down at the chalkboard sign. Today's pie special was Better Than Sex pie. I'd had it before and it was, indeed, better than any sex I'd ever had. Chocolate. Almonds. Coconuts. A trifecta for the taste buds. I hoped she was bringing me a piece.

Sure enough, Tookie returned a moment later with a huge slab of pie in a small cardboard to-go box. "On the house."

"Thanks, Tookie." As I took the container from her, the diamond on my engagement ring glinted in the sun. The stone was tiny, the ring cheap. It was all Allen could afford at the time, and I'd been thrilled to accept it. My wedding band had been inexpensive too, simple and plain. Allen had offered to replace the rings with a prettier, pricier set many times over the years, usually for our anniversary, but I'd always declined. I'd liked that the rings reflected who we'd been when we'd married—young, barely scraping by, crazy in love. They'd shown how far we'd come. Now, of course, we'd come to an end.

I debated what to do. Should I go home, take the day off, and have a good cry? Dull my pain with a bottle of pinot? Pile Allen's belongings on the front lawn, douse them with lighter fluid, and start a bonfire? Tempting as these ideas were, I had work to do and I'd be damned if I let that cheating son-of-a-bitch jeopardize my business reputation.

Rather than seek immediate solace or revenge, I turned and headed to Tumbleweed Pawn & Pistol. The shop was a mom-and-pop operation, with Warren and Sharon Stockton calling the shots. The couple employed their three adult sons. The trio were named after gun brands—Remington, Winchester, and Ruger—though the first two went by the nicknames Remi and Chester for short. It goes without saying that the Stocktons were gun nuts, though here I've gone and said it anyway.

While oil towns like Tumbleweed experienced boom and bust cycles, the Stocktons' business was always booming. When the economy was doing well, customers came in to buy their wares. When the economy was in the toilet, residents came in to pawn items for cash to pay their bills. In hopes of expanding the store, Warren and Sharon had applied for the bank loan. Though their business had been very profitable, they didn't have much in the way of liquid assets. Their sons had been prolific procreators. There wasn't much to do in Tumbleweed and, when residents got bored, they either turned to each other or on each other. Someone was always getting knocked up or knocked down. The Stocktons boasted a dozen grandchildren, each of whom they spoiled rotten. If they'd listened to my advice, they'd have put more of their earnings into their IRAs and investment accounts rather than into video game systems, Barbie Dream Houses, and annual trips to Disney World, but I couldn't blame them for wanting to show their grandkids some love.

The store had just opened for business and no customers were yet in the shop. I passed the display of assorted used tablets and cell phones. Older generation iPads and iPhones. A couple of Android devices. All were plugged into a long power strip so that they'd be fully charged if a customer wanted to check out their features. I continued on past the display of power tools and luggage until I reached the checkout desk.

Sharon stood behind the counter, putting the day's start-up cash in the till. Her wavy hair was dyed a shiny black, much too dark to be natural at her age, but it was nonetheless attractive. Heck, I dyed my hair, too. She wore light makeup in neutral shades on her heart-shaped face, and a pair of readers perched halfway down her nose.

Sharon smiled when she saw me come inside. "Hello, Debbie. Here about the audit?"

"No," I said, "though it's the first thing on my to-do list for today." I stepped up to the counter, set my pie down, and tugged the rings off my finger. I weighed twenty-five pounds more than I had when Allen and I had married all those years ago, and the rings fit much tighter now. Once I managed to pull the rings off, I placed them on the counter. "How much can I get for these rings? I'm not looking for a loan. I want to sell them outright."

"Uh-oh." Sharon picked up the engagement ring and eyed me through the hole. "Trouble in paradise?"

"Allen and I are splitting up."

"I see."

Fortunately, she didn't push for details. Surely, she'd seen many desperate people walk through her doors. The pawn shop business model was based on desperation, in fact. The store provided loans to people unable to obtain funds through more conventional means. She must have heard many a sob story over the years. My story was so common it wouldn't even be interesting. *Man goes through mid-life crises, cheats on wife with younger woman, blah-blah-blah.*

The bells on the door jingled behind me as another customer came into the store. Ruger turned around from the guitar display. His hair was every bit as dark and shiny as his mother's, though his color was still natural. His eyes were dark, too, like strong coffee, so dark, in fact, that the pupils got lost in them. Ruger had played linebacker for the high school football team, and bore the big, broad shoulders of a gorilla. He gave me a nod in greeting, and I returned the gesture.

As her son walked over to help the customer, Sharon reached into a drawer behind the counter and pulled out a jeweler's loupe to take a better look at the diamond. Peering through the small lens, she angled the ring to and fro to get a complete look. Meanwhile, I took a look at my bare ring finger. The skin where my rings had been was pale and moist. I wondered how long it would take before it would no longer be obvious that I'd recently removed my rings.

After examining the engagement ring, Sharon set it back down, picked up the wedding band, and looked it over, too. She placed the band back on the counter and looked up at me. "I can give you two-hundred dollars for the set."

I knew she'd turn around and sell the rings for at least double that price, but I didn't take the lowball offer personally. The markup is how the Stocktons made their living. Besides, if I didn't sell the rings here, I'd have to place a listing online or drive to a bigger city. Both options would cost money and time, and I had no interest in doing either. "Sold."

Warren Stockton walked out of the storage room with a carton of ammunition. He was an older version of Ruger, a silverback gorilla, still formidable despite being eligible for social security. "Hey, Debbie."

"Hi, Warren," I said. "You doin' all right?"

"Never better. Took my youngest grandson on his first fishing trip last weekend down in Balmorhea. He caught himself two largemouth bass and a catfish." He pulled out his phone and swiped the screen to show me a series of photos of him and his grandson.

"That boy's a cutie."

"Yup," Warren agreed, tucking his phone back into the pocket of his jeans. "I suppose we'll keep 'im."

Warren headed over to stock the bullets in the display, and Sharon pushed a form across the counter to me. While I filled out the form, she proceeded to clean the rings with jewelry cleaner and a soft cloth until they gleamed, looking good as new. I couldn't remember the last time I'd bothered to clean my rings. It had probably been a decade or longer. I returned the form to her and accepted the two-hundred dollars in cash she handed me.

"You take care, now." She reached down and unlocked the jewelry case to add my wedding set to the available inventory.

I bade her goodbye, as well, and aimed for the door.

My left hand now bare, I walked the short distance to my CPA office, which was situated on the other side of the square. The building was aged reddish brick, chipped and scarred from centuries of use. The wide plate-glass window across the front of my space let in lots of natural light and offered a nice view of the square. I unlocked the glass door and stepped inside. After stowing my pie in the office mini-fridge, I locked the door again, rounded up my secondhand Lexus from its reserved parking spot out front, and drove to the house that, until this morning, I'd shared with Allen.

Buddha, my fat orange tabby, was lounging in a sunny spot on the living room floor. He raised his head and cocked it, surprised to see me back home so soon.

I reached down and ruffled his ears. "Hey, boy. You and I are moving out. Turns out that Allen's a cheating bastard."

Buddha followed me as I scurried around the house. I gathered my clothing, toiletries, to-be-read book pile, and the framed photos of our daughter. They were the only things I truly cared about. Allen could keep everything else. I didn't want anything that would remind me of him or our time together. It would be too painful. I'd rather make a fresh start.

Even so, I wasn't above a few petty acts of vengeance to even the score a little. I erased the latest shows he'd taped on the DVR and been planning to watch this evening. I poured out his bottle of Gentlemen Jack Whiskey. I set the alarm on the bedside clock to go off at two A.M.

When I was done, I glanced around the house one last time, bidding it a silent goodbye. I scooped up my cat and slid him into his plastic carrier to take with me. I drove back to my CPA office, and parked once again in my reserved parking space in front of my office. A bright red bicycle was chained to the sign that read RESERVED FOR DEBRA OTT, CPA. My intern, a bright and promising college student, had arrived while I'd been busy being an unwitting voyeur at my husband's office and packing my things at my house.

I carried Buddha and my now-cold latte into the office with me. The space was small, fifteen feet wide and twenty feet deep, but 300 square feet of space was big enough for a solo practitioner and an assistant, especially now that data and files were stored electronically rather than in filing cabinets. The interior walls were exposed brick, same as the outside, though the wall dividing my office from the reception area in front was standard drywall painted robin's egg blue with white trim.

Arielle looked up from her antique desk. Ari was a lean and petite young black woman, with an abundance of natural curls framing her face. Not only was she an honor student—I would hire no less—she played softball for the West Texas Ferals. Her college T-shirt read WTF across the chest. Her smile faltered when she saw my face. "Debit? Are you okay?"

"I will be," I said, my voice quavering. "It just might take a little time." I set Buddha's carrier atop the coffee table and released him before turning to her. "I caught my husband this morning in flagrante delicto."

"Is that the new deli on Third Street? Word on the street is they serve great potato salad."

"No, it means—"

She gave me a patient smile. "I know what it means, Deb. I was just trying to lighten the mood."

I sighed. "Thanks, Ari. It almost worked." I flopped back on the faux-leather sofa and it released a disgusting farting sound. Brrrrt. *This is proving to be quite a day.* I took a sip of my cold latte and cringed.

Arielle rose from her rolling chair and circled around her desk. "Let me warm that up for you."

I gave her an appreciative smile. "What did I do to deserve you?"

She arched a brow. "You remember you pay me, right?"

"And here I was, thinking you were sweet and thoughtful," I teased. "I won't make that mistake again."

She took my cup and walked it over to nuke it in the microwave we kept on a stand in the corner next to the mini fridge. While she warmed my coffee, I retrieved the pie from the refrigerator, cut it down the middle, and slid it onto two small paper plates. I rounded up two forks, as well.

When the microwave dinged, Ari handed the warm cup back to me, and I traded it for half the pie. She took a seat at her desk and I returned to the sofa.

Ari dug into her pie, moaning in bliss much like Allen and his auburn-haired lover had been moaning this morning. "I don't know what Tookie puts in her pies," Ari said, "but I'm pretty sure it's magic."

I took a couple of bites of my slice and wiped my mouth. "I'll need to find somewhere to live until I can figure things out." My daughter would let me crash in her guest room if I asked, but I didn't want to put her in the middle. "You know any place around town that's for lease?" With her being a college student, she might be in the know about apartments or maybe a duplex for rent.

She pointed upward. "The studio upstairs is available."

"It is?"

She nodded. "I saw someone putting up a for rent sign this morning."

My office was in one of the oldest buildings on the square, and had been constructed in an era when many shopkeepers lived above their stores. "I'll check it out." I whipped out my phone and texted the building's owner, who was also my landlord for my CPA office. Can I take a look at the studio upstairs?

She responded right away. Of course. The code for the lockbox is 2315. Just put the key back in the lockbox when you're done.

"I'm going up to take a look," I told Arielle. "Want to come up with me? I'd love to get your opinion."

She shrugged. "Sure."

I'd also like Buddha's opinion. I scooped him up in my arms to take him with us.

I jotted a quick message on a sticky note—*We'll be right back!*—and attached it to the glass on the front door of my office. We exited, locked the office door, and walked twenty feet down to a second door. Unlike the glass door of my office, this door was solid wood with a peephole in it, similar to the front door on most houses. A sign tacked to it read STUDIO APT FOR RENT, along with my landlord's phone number. I tucked Buddha under one arm and turned the dials on the lockbox until they read 2315. The box popped open, allowing me access to the key.

I unlocked the door to find a narrow staircase that led up to a landing on the second floor. The same key that had opened the lower door also opened the door to the apartment. The size of the unit mirrored that of my office below, a mere three-hundred square feet. The décor could best be described as fresh-from-a-curb, but the space had everything one person and her cat would need. A horseshoe-shaped kitchen that looked out over the square, along with a bistro set with mismatched chairs for eating. A small living space with a threadbare tweed loveseat and a lopsided recliner on either side of a scarred wood coffee table. A queen-sized bed sat at the back of the space, flanked on one side by a dresser and the other by a night table on which sat a lamp shaped like a prickly pear cactus. The bathroom had a pedestal sink, toilet, and an original clawfoot tub.

"Ooooh!" Ari squealed, clapping her hands at her chest. "That tub will be great for soaking in. An hour in a hot bath with some lavender oil and you'll forget you ever knew your husband."

Buddha sniffed his way around the space before leaping up onto the kitchen counter. He looked down on the activity in the square for a moment or two, then settled down on his haunches, already at home at his new viewing post.

I glanced around then looked up at the ceiling for any evidence of leaks. I saw no tell-tale water marks on the wooden ceiling, but I did see a short rope hanging down, marking the entrance to a pull-down attic. I pulled down on the rope until the hatch opened, revealing a folding ladder. After tugging the ladder into place, I climbed up just far enough that I could see into the attic space. Dim light shined through vents under the eaves of the building, and I supplemented the illumination with my cell phone flashlight. Though there was plenty of dust and cobwebs in the attic, it was otherwise empty. I saw no droppings or other evidence of rodents. *Good.*

I descended the ladder, closed the hatch, and texted my landlord. How much is the rent?

She texted back. $600/mo. Six-month lease minimum.

I responded with: I'll pay $550 on a month-to-month basis.

After a little more back and forth, we split the difference and settled on $575 and a three-month lease. *I hope my divorce will be settled this quickly and easily.*

CHAPTER 2
GOD, GUNS, AND GLORY

ARIELLE HELPED me carry my personal things from my car up to the apartment. It took all of twenty minutes for me to establish my new home. I supposed there'd be a few things I'd need to pick up at the store—dishes, pots and pans, towels, and cleaning supplies—but I could take care of the shopping this evening. For now, I needed to get back downstairs and get to work.

My assistant and I returned to the office and took seats at our respective desks, hers in the front and mine in the back. I left the door to my office open so that I could communicate easily with Ari and enjoy the view through the front windows. The pink granite courthouse loomed over the square along with a statue of Ranger Spurr in his Texas Rangers uniform. The rear windows in my office looked out on an alley filled with trash dumpsters and fire escapes, which is why I kept the curtains closed. Nobody wants to see a smelly garbage truck rumble by.

With the seasonal tax rush now wrapped up, it was on to other financial matters. The largest of the projects I'd tackle now would be the audit of Tumbleweed Pawn & Pistols. My audit process would involve verifying a sample of the shop's accounts and reviewing their internal accounting controls to ensure they had reasonable safeguards in place to reduce the likelihood of financial shenanigans. After performing the analysis, I would issue an opinion on the financial statements that would be presented to the bank's underwriters. My clients and the bank expected a "clean" or "unqualified" opinion, which would state that I had found the financial statements to be accurate in all material respects.

More than half of Tumbleweed Pawn & Pistol's business involved gun sales. This was Texas, after all, where every Tom and hairy Dick could amass a personal armory with little to no regulation by the state. Ironically, while I could run down to the pawn shop right now and come out with a gun in each hand, I hadn't been able to adopt Buddha from the city pound without first filling out a detail application, providing references, and registering for a pet license. Texas lawmakers seemed more concerned about mass shedding than mass shootings. *Don't even get me started …*

At any rate, audits involved reviewing the client's financial records, of course, but they also involved verifying accounts receivable and accounts payable with third parties. In order to verify the amounts purportedly due for gun orders the Stocktons had placed, I'd prepare letters to be mailed to a sample of vendors. Audits didn't require that every number be verified, only that a big enough statistical sample be analyzed that the odds of widespread misstatement was unlikely.

I used the password Sharon Stockton had given me to log into their QuickBooks account, which they maintained online. I ran my eyes down the list of vendors who supplied guns to the store. There were just over twenty of them. *Five would be a good-sized sample for the audit.* I chose the vendors at random. Amarillo Ammo and Firearms Corporation, Maverick Riflery Corp., Big D Gun Depot Inc., Hunter Outfitters Corp., and High Falutin' Shootin' Supply Incorporated.

I looked through the vendor invoices to match them to the data that had been inputted into the system, making sure the amounts on the invoices matched the amounts actually paid to the vendors. Once I'd verified the figures, I harvested the vendors' addresses from the mastheads on the invoices—for all but Big D Gun Depot, anyway. Oddly, the invoices from Big D Gun Depot provided no physical or mailing address. No phone number or e-mail address, either. *Hmm.* I ran my eyes down the list of items purchased. Per the invoice, all of the guns were used inventory, not new. Nothing unusual about that. Pawn shops dealt in primarily secondhand property.

After some poking around, I found Big D's mailing address in the vendor account profile. Sharon handled bookkeeping for the pawn shop. She must have input Big D's contact information into the bookkeeping system.

I forwarded the gun companies' addresses to Ari via e-mail, along with the amount of the outstanding account payable to each gun wholesaler, so that she could prepare letters for my signature. The largest balance due was to Big D in the amount of $18,365.74. The letters would be simple and straightforward, instructing the gun dealers to check one of two boxes to indicate whether the stated account balance was correct—yes or no. After checking the appropriate box, they were to return the letter to me in the self-addressed stamped envelope provided to them.

As Ari prepared the letters at her desk, I moved on to the pawn shop's other accounts. As one of the few CPAs in town, I could verify many of the accounts from information already in my system. Tumbleweed Pawn & Pistols paid a local security company a monthly fee for an alarm system and monitoring. Because I also prepared the security company's tax returns, all I had to do to verify the fees was consult the security company's records. Same for their office supplies account, most of which were basic items purchased at a local store for which I also prepared income tax, payroll, and sales tax returns. Next, I took a quick moment to review the pawn shop's payroll account. Because I prepared individual tax returns for all of the Stockton family, I had access to the W-2s the business had issued to them. *Yep. Everything checks out.*

Ari stepped into my office carrying the prepared letters for me to sign. She slid the stack onto my desk in front of me.

I whipped out a pen and signed each of them in turn before handing them back to her for mailing. "When you mail them, don't forget to include the S.A.S.E."

"I W.O.N.T.," she said.

"Watch it, sassypants." I fought a grin. Truth be told, her feisty, spirited demeanor made the office more fun. Besides, she knew when to behave. She was the consummate professional on the phone and when clients were in the office. The last college student who'd worked for me had been devoid of personality. Though she'd been a hard worker, she'd been a total bore. I'd been glad when she'd graduated and moved to Houston to work for a larger firm and I'd found the livelier Arielle to replace her.

Arielle stopped in the doorway and turned back to me. "You should get on those dating apps, find yourself a new, better man."

"It's too soon," I said.

"No, it's not. Your marriage is over right? Life's short. Why wait? Get back on that horse."

"I haven't even told my husband I'm leaving him or had time to call a divorce lawyer." *I suppose I'd better hire one quick.* In a town the size of Tumbleweed, there were only a handful of attorneys who handled family law matters. I wanted to make sure I hired the best of them.

As Ari returned to her desk, I pulled up my browser, typed in divorce lawyers Tumbleweed, Texas, and consulted their rankings and reviews. I grabbed the receiver of my desk phone and dialed the one with the highest ranking, a 4.9 out of 5. She was described as fair, firm, and unflappable, just what I wanted in my legal representation. Despite Allen's cheating, I didn't want to take him to the cleaners. I just wanted everything we'd amassed over the years to be split down the middle. Texas was a community property state, after all, and even though Allen earned more than me now, I'd put the guy through dental school. He wouldn't be where he was now if it wasn't for me.

A receptionist answered the phone, consulted the attorney's schedule and, in less than a minute, I had an appointment set for Friday in the early afternoon. I supposed I'd need to collect my personal financial information to turn over to her.

As I hung up the phone, I realized that my fury at Allen had already begun to dissipate. I still felt angry, but other feelings had displaced some of that anger. I felt surprisingly light and free, as if released from a prison of my own making. I'd once loved Allen, but seeing him screwing that patient forced me to face the truth, and the truth was I'd just been going through the motions for years now. I supposed he had, too. Still, I would never have crossed the line like he had, not without a formal separation. I had too much integrity.

I turned back to my computer. Rather than digging further into the pawn shop's records, I sat and pondered for a moment. Maybe Ari was right. Maybe I should put a profile on a dating app. *What do I have to lose?* I decided to look into a site for people over fifty. I was no cougar, looking for a boy toy. If I was going to date, I wanted a man with some miles on him, like me. I searched online for options. There was a site called OurTime, which I'd seen ads for on TV. Another was called SilverSingles. A third site, Second-Chance Romance, was designed specifically for adults over fifty who'd been married before but were now widowed or divorced. I decided to give that one a try.

I filled out the questionnaire on the website and uploaded

a profile pic of me wearing sneakers, jeans, and a shapeless sweater, while holding Buddha on my lap. I refused to upload a sexy photo. Hell, I didn't even have a sexy photo of myself. And if any potential matches didn't like cats or cat ladies, it was best to let them know up front I was not the woman for them. Next, the system asked me to write a short profile in which I described myself and what I was looking for. After much typing, deleting, and revision, I eventually came up with: *I am a financial professional and avid reader. Looking for an intelligent, easygoing companion.* It was simple and straightforward. I was curious to see who, if anyone, would respond.

CHAPTER 3
HUNTING FOR A GUN DEALER

MY MEETING with the divorce attorney was short. I gave her a quick rundown. *Married thirty years, caught husband cheating, don't want to punish him for being an idiot but won't settle for less than half of everything.* He could keep the house if he wanted it, but he'd have to pay me fifty-percent of the equity we'd accrued.

She gave me a curt nod. "Sounds more than reasonable." I handed her the financial paperwork. She set it on her desk and riffled through it before looking back up at me. "You're way ahead of the game here. This information will enable me to get started on the property settlement proposal right away. I can have your petition for divorce filed tomorrow morning."

"Fantastic." No need to wait. I wouldn't be changing my mind. I preferred to treat my marriage like a facial wax and rip it off as quickly as possible.

Allen appeared to feel the same. He hadn't begged me to take him back, though he had apologized via text after I'd refused to answer his many phone calls. *I'm so sorry, Deb. There's no excuse for what I did. I didn't want you to see that.* I hadn't wanted to see him screwing another woman, either. *Had his ass always been so saggy?* I supposed I couldn't be too harsh. Middle age had ravaged my body, too, and gravity had taken a toll. Nothing was up where it used to be. Still, I was lucky. I suffered from no major health issues. I'd count my blessings.

————

I invited my daughter and her husband out for dinner at a Mexican restaurant Friday evening. I knew I had to tell Hayleigh about the divorce, but I feared the breakup might upset her, make her question the strength of her own marriage. I hoped it wouldn't. Over chips, salsa, and frozen margaritas, I attempted to gently break the news. "You might have noticed that your father and I have grown apart over the years. I—"

"Filed for divorce?" Hayleigh asked, nonchalantly taking a sip of her margarita.

"Yes." I cocked my head. "You don't seem upset."

She used a tortilla chip to scoop up a huge blob of guacamole. "Because I saw this coming a mile away."

"You did?"

"Yeah. You two spend way more time with your friends than with each other."

She wasn't wrong. I enjoyed my monthly book club and frequent girls' nights out with my female friends, though I supposed we hardly qualified as "girls" anymore. Allen had preferred to golf all day on the weekends to doing anything with me, and I hadn't minded his absence one bit. On the contrary, I'd enjoyed the quiet alone time at the house. Our needs had changed over time, and different people fulfilled those needs.

I gave my daughter a soft smile. "Well, you made this easy."

She raised her margarita glass. "You've got to give some credit to José Cuervo."

"To José," I said, lifting my glass as well. "And to new beginnings."

Her husband raised his glass, too, and we tapped them against each other. "To new beginnings," they said.

———

I spent the weekend pampering myself and allowing myself to grieve the death of my marriage. Even though I knew divorcing Allen was the right thing to do, I felt sad that the love he and I had once shared had died, that I'd spent so many years in a marriage that had been over long ago. I gave myself a mani-pedi and a facial. I deep conditioned my hair. I took a long soak in the tub like Ari had suggested. Buddha sat on the toilet lid, watching me. I reached out a wet, lavender-scented hand to pet him. Big mistake. I ended up with a handful of orange fur stuck to my skin.

Late Saturday afternoon, my phone pinged. My heart performed a flip when I consulted the screen. The dating app had sent a notification that I'd made a possible match in Tumbleweed.

I logged into the website to take a look at my cyber suitor. I recognized the photo instantly. The man was a client. I'd prepared his tax returns and knew he earned good money. I also knew he'd filed jointly over the years with no less than five wives in fairly rapid succession. I wasn't looking for a commitment, but I also wasn't looking for someone unable to maintain one. *Been there, done that.* Looked like I'd need to expand my search radius if I wanted more options. I modified my acceptable geographic range to include men within a hundred miles of Tumbleweed.

News traveled fast in T-Weed. A neighbor who'd seen me carrying my things out to my car had told a friend, who'd told a friend, who told my friend Terry, a real estate agent, that I'd moved out. Before I could even get around to calling her, she'd called me to find out what was going on. Terry rounded up the gang and they showed up at my apartment Saturday night with wine, snacks, a shoofly pie from Tookie's diner, and the latest board game. We gathered around the tiny coffee table, some of us sitting on the floor. It felt like a high school slumber party.

Terry glanced around the place, her nose quirking in distaste. "In the real estate biz, we'd describe this studio as 'a cozy space with retro charm.' How long is your lease?"

"Three months," I said. "I hope to be in my own house by then. Know of any nice properties for sale? Something I could manage on my own?"

"A three-bedroom, two-bath brick home just came on the market today. It's just one block over from your daughter's place. The husband works for an oil company and got transferred to Houston. It's priced to sell. I can show it to you first thing tomorrow."

"Perfect."

Terry sipped her merlot, rolled the dice, and moved her game piece down the board before eyeing me more intently. "How are you holding up, Deb? Are you lonely?"

"It's only been a few days. I'm still working through it." I picked up the dice and shook them. "But, no, I'm not lonely. I've got Buddha to keep me company."

"A cat can make a good companion, that's true." Terry leaned in and said, "But what about your other needs?"

"What other needs?"

"You know," she said in a stage whisper everyone could hear. "Your *carnal* needs."

"I'm menopausal. I have carnal needs only once per quarter, just like estimated taxes."

She sighed. "That's just sad."

When the others murmured in agreement, I whipped out my phone to show them my dating app. "Look. I've put myself out there. Does that make you happy?"

Terry took my phone from me and sipped her wine as she read over my profile. She shook her head. "Your profile is too sterile. You need to state who you really are and what you truly want."

"You mean something like - *I'm a successful lady boss seeking a man with a one-percenter income and twelve-inch cock to shower me with gifts and provide hours of carnal pleasure*?"

"Exactly."

"A one-percenter with a long dong is not what I'm actually looking for." *Well, maybe the long dong.* "I don't really care what a man earns, so long as he's making ends meet and not looking for a handout from me. What I really want at this point in my life is a man to have occasional casual fun with, one who makes me laugh or think or introduces me to new things. No strings attached."

She looked up in thought, then her fingers moved over my screen. She handed the phone back to me. She'd edited my profile to read *Back on the market! I'm an attractive, newly single self-employed financial professional who enjoys crime novels, jamming to 80's music, and weekend road trips. Looking for a handsome, smart, self-sufficient man to share some casual fun. Make me laugh, make me think, or make me dinner. No mama's boys.*

She cocked her head. "What do you think?"

"I think it's worth a shot." I set my phone on the table and we resumed playing the game.

In minutes, my phone dinged with a response. A man had expressed interest in meeting me. I held up my phone to show my friends his profile pic.

"He's handsome," Terry said. "Swipe right."

"It'll never work," I said. "His profile says he's an oil company executive. I drive a hybrid car, remember?" That earth-friendly choice had earned me some rude comments from Tumbleweeders who toiled in the oil and gas industry. Never mind that fossil fuels were responsible for the climate change that had caused the recent blizzard, deemed "Snowmageddon," that had left people without power, food, or water for days.

I swiped left and we continued the game.

At the end of the night, I gave each of them a goodbye hug at the street-level door downstairs. "Thanks so much for coming by." Their support had helped me realize I would be fine on my own. "Y'all are the best."

————

Terry showed me the house Sunday morning. It was a cute one-story model, a manageable fourteen-hundred square feet with a covered patio that would be perfect for a chaise lounge I could relax on for reading. The place could use a fresh coat of paint both in and out, as well as new carpet, but there was plenty of time remaining on my apartment lease to get the improvements done before I moved in. Given Buddha's propensity to hack up hairballs, I might even opt for hardwoods throughout. I could also use the time to buy some new furniture. I made an offer, went back and forth with the sellers on the price and a few other particulars, and eventually came to a mutually acceptable agreement. Terry scheduled an inspection for later in the week. With any luck, the inspector would find no major problems and we could move forward.

Over the next few days, letters were returned from the gun vendors and other parties to whom I'd sent inquiries in order to verify the account balances shown in the pawn shop's financial records. All but one letter, anyway.

Late Thursday morning, the bells on the office door jangled as the mail carrier entered with his bag. He handed a stack of mail to Ari and raised a hand in greeting to me. I raised a hand and offered a smile in return before he hustled out to continue on his rounds.

Ari sorted through the mail, dropping most of it into the

recycle bin but carrying the rest of it into my office. She placed all but one envelope in my inbox. She frowned and held up the remaining envelope. "The letter to Big D Gun Depot was returned."

I reached out to take the envelope from her. The post office had stamped the front with the words NO SUCH ADDRESS in red ink. *Hmm.* This was a teachable moment. I looked up at Ari. "Pull up a chair. I'll teach you some tricks of the trade."

She grabbed a chair from my small conference table and rolled it up next to my desk chair.

"First, let's check the address and make sure the mail was correctly returned. It's possible there was an error at the post office." To that end, I pulled up the United States Postal Service zip code lookup and typed in the address. The website returned a message in red: *Unfortunately, this information wasn't found. Please double-check it and try again.*

Arielle read the screen. "That confirms the address is invalid, doesn't it?"

"Looks that way," I said, "but just to be sure let me see if my GPS can locate it." I pulled out my cell phone and typed the address into my maps app. It brought up a similar address, but not the one I was looking for. I then simply typed the address into my browser on my computer. The search returned nothing useful.

Ari mimicked the sound of a game show wrong-answer buzzer. "*Eeert!* Looks like the address is definitely wrong."

"I agree. Let's see if we can track down the company." I went through my usual process. First, I searched online for a website. But when I typed the name of the company into my browser, no link for a company website popped up.

Ari leaned in to look at my screen. "That's weird, isn't it? I mean, what business doesn't have a website these days?"

"It's unexpected, yeah." Websites were cheap and vital, and numerous do-it-yourself systems were available for those who didn't want to pay a professional web designer. Even so, there were still a few small or specialized operations that didn't find them necessary. *A gun dealer, though? In Texas? Seems it would have a site.* "Maybe the company has been bought out. Or maybe it changed names."

I showed Ari how to log into the Comptroller of Public Accounts site and search for business entities registered with the state. Nothing came up when I searched for Big D Gun Depot. I tried Big D Gun. Still nothing. Then I tried simply Big D. While that search returned a number of businesses with Big D in their name, none appeared to have anything to do with guns. Things were getting stranger by the moment.

Ari jotted some notes on her legal pad so she'd know how to run a search like this herself next time. "What now?"

"We're going to have to make a good, old-fashioned phone call."

She rolled her eyes. "Ugh. Talking to people is so last century."

I dialed the number for the Texas Secretary of State's Corporations Division and put the call on speaker so Ari could listen in. After holding for a minute or two, a representative answered the call. "How can I help you?"

"I'm trying to locate a business," I said. "It goes by the name Big D Gun Depot. It's purportedly incorporated."

The rep ran a search. "I'm getting nothing under that name. Let me try some variations." Just like I'd done, he attempted to find the business under a similar name. Also like me, he had no luck. "I'm getting no results. Sorry."

"Thanks for your time." I ended the call and turned to Ari. "There's one last place we can look." I logged into the Dallas County Clerk's website and searched the assumed names records. An assumed name was a business name used by an individual who didn't want to operate under their own name. This search was a last-ditch effort and it, too, yielded no results. I frowned. "It's as if this business doesn't exist."

Ari said, "But the pawn shop has bought guns from Big D before, right? How did they pay for them?"

I pulled up the shop's records and looked through the transactions. "They paid Big D via Venmo." Unfortunately, all I could glean from the Venmo receipts was Big D Gun Depot's user name. No other contact information appeared on their profile. "We've done what we can. Let's give Sharon Stockton a call."

As before, I left the phone on speaker so Ari could listen in on the conversation.

When the phone was answered, a male voice came over the line. "Tumbleweed Pawn and Pistols. Remi speaking. What can I do you for?"

I identified myself and asked if Sharon was available. "I've got a quick question for the audit."

"All righty," Remi replied. "I'll transfer you back to Mom's desk."

He put us on hold. Rather than music, their system played a recording of Warren Stockton shamelessly promoting the store. *Want a guitar? We got 'em! Television? We got those, too! Need a gun? Get on down here and check out our extensive inventory of firearms. We've got everything from the smallest of handguns for little ladies to long-range hunting rifles for you men. Best prices in town, too!*

Ari scoffed and muttered, "Little ladies? That's so sexist."

After a few more seconds, Warren was silenced when Sharon came on the line. "Hi, Deb. I was told you had a question about the audit?"

"That's right. I'm having trouble tracking down Big D Gun Depot. A letter I sent to them was marked 'no such address.' I've confirmed that the address listed in your bookkeeping system isn't an actual address. Do you know where you got that address?"

"I can't recall. Probably off an invoice."

"That's the thing. Their invoices don't show an address. The only information on them is the name of the company."

Her voice rose in surprise. "Really?"

"Really. Take a look at the copies in your purchase records and you'll see."

"Huh," she said. "I hadn't noticed."

"Do you happen to have an e-mail address or phone number for them?"

"No e-mail," she said. "They only take orders by phone."

What business doesn't communicate by e-mail, at least regarding routine matters, such as the status of an order? "That's unusual, isn't it?"

"I suppose they want to cultivate relationships with their customers, provide more personalized service," she surmised. "That's hard to do via e-mail. I'm sure I've got Big D Gun Depot's business card around here somewhere. Hold on a second and let me see what I can scrounge up."

Sharon put us on hold, and there was a rustling noise before she returned to the line. "I've found the business card Chester got from Big D's rep at the gun show in Fort Worth. How about I text you the image?"

"That would be great," I said. "Front and back."

"The back is blank."

"Text it anyway," I said. "I'll need it for my records."

"Okey doke."

We ended the call, and a few seconds later my cell phone pinged as the pics came through. The business card provided no website for the store, no physical or mailing address, and no name for the salesperson Chester had met at the gun show. All the card provided was the name of the business and a phone number, along with the slogan *We do business the old-fashioned way, person-to-person with a handshake.* A bit hokey, sure, but some people liked things that way.

I dialed the number on the card. An outgoing message said, "Thank you for calling Big D Gun Depot. Sorry we missed you. We're either on another call or servicing another customer. Please leave your name, number, and tell us what you're in the market for, and we'll get back to you as soon as possible."

After the *beeeep*, I left a message identifying myself, explaining that I needed them to verify sales to Tumbleweed Pawn and Pistols, and asked for someone in their accounting department to call me back. I sighed as I returned the receiver to the cradle and turned to Arielle. "I hope we'll hear from them soon. The rest of the audit is nearly done. This could hold things up." At least my divorce was moving along. Allen had agreed to all of my terms. Our property would be split fifty-fifty. He'd remain in the house and would buy out my share of the equity. He even offered to throw in an extra ten grand for my half of the furniture and household effects. The ten grand would furnish my new house. *He must be feeling guilty. Good. He deserves to suffer a little.*

CHAPTER 4
IMPASSE

WHEN I DIDN'T HEAR BACK from Big D Gun Depot by Friday morning, I left another voicemail. Over the weekend, I spent some time at a local furniture store. I found a bedroom suite that I liked, and ordered a queen-sized mattress set to go with it. Most of their living room sets were leather or faux-leather, oversized and masculine styles. I wanted my new place to fit my taste, to feature bright colors and feminine touches. Looked like I'd have to drive to Midland or El Paso to see more options. I didn't quite trust ordering furniture online. I wanted to give it a personal comfort test before purchasing.

On Monday, Sharon Stockton called to find out why I hadn't issued my audit opinion yet. "We need to get moving on the expansion. What's the hold-up?"

"I'm still waiting to hear from Big D Gun Depot," I explained. "I've left them several messages, but I'll call them again."

"You do that," Sharon said, sounding none too happy. "We're running out of time. The contractor says if we don't get the loan and pay one-third down by the end of the week, he's going to have to start another project. The expansion could be delayed by months."

"That's unfortunate," I said. "If I have to leave a message for Big D again, I'll be sure to emphasize that time is of the essence."

The instant Sharon and I ended our call, I phoned Big D. As before, I reached no human being, and my call was routed to voicemail. "This matter is extremely urgent," I said. "My clients can't move forward with their expansion until I hear back from you. Please call me right away."

Still, my call wasn't returned.

———

On Tuesday afternoon, while Ari was attending a class, I jotted a message on a sticky note and affixed it to the front door of my office. **I'll be back by 3:00.** I had no appointments, but occasionally clients stopped by for a quick question or to ask for a copy of something from their tax records. Couldn't hurt to let them know when I'd return.

While my office was on the western side of the square, the pawn shop sat on the eastern side. I slung my tote bag over my shoulder, locked the door to my office, and headed across the square. The smell of freshly brewed coffee wafted over from the Cowboy Coffee Shop, competing with the enticing aroma of fried foods and onions drifting from Tookie's Diner. *I know where I'm having dinner tonight.*

A bird sat atop the Ranger Spurr statue. Ranger Spurr had been one of the town's early residents, and its first shop-keeper. Local historians maintained he'd also been a pimp, running a brothel in the space over his mercantile. Spurr's descendants rabidly disputed this fact. However, the financial records for the mercantile, which were on display on the local history museum, contained cryptic entries for purchases of "fresh fruit" by customers identified only by codenames. The customers paid handsomely for "peaches," "watermelons," and "cantaloupes," far above market price at the time for the actual fruits. As they say, numbers don't lie.

Mischief-makers had adorned the former Texas Ranger with an assortment of accessories. He sported a hot-pink bra, a set of shiny Mardi Gras beads, and an elastic garter on his thigh. Locals treated the statue like a dress-up doll. But who could blame them? There wasn't much to do out here in the barren lands of west Texas. People had to make their own fun. As I approached the statue, the bird cawed, dropped a white load of poop on the man's ranger hat and flew off.

I continued on, looking both ways before jaywalking across the street to the Pawn & Pistols. As I entered the pawn shop, muted classic country music met my ears. It was an old Waylon Jennings' tune. *Damn that man had a deep, sexy voice.* I wouldn't mind a manly voice like that whispering sweet nothings into my ear. It had been a while.

Remi was busy showing a customer an electronic keyboard, while Chester rang up another customer at the register. The two were virtual clones of Ruger—tall, dark, handsome, and hulking. After Chester completed the transaction, he handed the man a rifle with a scratched wooden stock, clearly a secondhand gun. The man carried it past me as he left the store. Though guns were ubiquitous in Texas, they still made me nervous—well, maybe not so much the guns, but the look of some of the people who carried them. Seriously, if someone can't be trusted to brush their teeth or comb their hair on a regular basis, they shouldn't be trusted with a deadly weapon.

I walked up to the counter. "Hey, Ruger. Your mother around?"

He hiked a thumb at a glass-paneled door behind him. "She's in her office. I'll let her know you're here." He picked up the receiver from a phone behind the counter and punched two buttons. "The accountant's here to see you." He listened for a beat, returned the phone to the cradle, and said, "You can go on back."

"Thanks." I circled around the counter. The glass panel in the window of Sharon's office was lined with one-way reflective film, allowing anyone inside to see out, but nobody on the outside could see in. It was probably a good way to keep an eye out for shoplifters. I eyed my reflection, feeling as if I was in a funhouse mirror maze, unable to distinguish who was real and who was merely an illusion. I opened the door and stepped inside, gently closing the door behind me. Sharon's large, windowless office was an organized mess of paperwork, office equipment, and pawned items in need of cleaning or repair. Assorted sized metal filing cabinets formed a skyline of sorts on the wall to the right. On a bookshelf to the left sat a dozen or more framed family photos. In many of them, the family members wore Mickey Mouse ears from one of their many trips to Orlando to meet the famous rodent.

Sharon sat in her cushy, high-backed rolling chair behind the desk. After we exchanged greetings, she offered me a seat and a cup of tea.

I took the seat, but not the tea. "No thanks. I've been drinking coffee all morning. Any more caffeine and I'll never sleep tonight."

"Okey doke." She angled her head. "You get the audit wrapped up?"

"No, unfortunately. I'm at an impasse. No matter what I do, I can't seem to get Big D Gun Depot to verify their account. The letter I mailed them was returned marked 'no such address', as I mentioned before. I've left them multiple voicemails, but nobody has returned my calls. They don't have a website as far as I can tell. I've searched state and local government filings. There's no business registered in that name. It's like they don't actually exist."

"A ghost company?" Sharon chuckled. "If that company

doesn't exist, where'd we get most of those guns out there?" She pointed out of the window of her office toward the extensive gun display. With a frustrated frown, she added, "I've sent a pretty penny to the company via Venmo. Multiple times. Somebody got those funds. They've always fulfilled our orders, too."

"Who delivers the guns to you?"

"They're shipped via UPS."

I hadn't yet thought to check the shipping records. "Do you have a copy of the shipping documents for a recent order?"

"I'm sure I do." She turned to her computer, worked her mouse and keyboard, and printed out a copy of the shipping agreement from the most recent delivery from Big D.

I ran my gaze over the document and noted that the address on the form matched the fictional address Sharon had given me earlier. Had someone made a typo along the way and failed to correct it? Or was something more dubious going on?

"The address on this shipping label isn't accurate." I told her everything I'd done to confirm that the address wasn't legit. I raised my hands in defeat, totally stumped. "I'm out of ideas."

She issued a *hmph* and pursed her lips, looking up in thought before returning her focus to me. "You said you don't have to verify accounts from all of our suppliers, right? That an audit is only a sampling? Just pick a different vendor to use in your sample."

"I wish it was that easy," I said. "But now that I'm aware of an issue, I have an ethical obligation to disclose that the account could not be verified. I'd be in violation of Generally Accepted Auditing Standards if I changed my sample without making the disclosure. I could also get in hot water with the State Board of Public Accountancy."

Sharon frowned. "If you can't do what we hired you to do,

which was to issue an unqualified opinion on our financials, then we'll have to hire another CPA who will."

My temperature skyrocketed. I was insulted, sure, but I was also concerned. "Hiring a different accountant won't solve the problem. That's called 'opinion shopping.' Your new CPA would be required to disclose that you've engaged in the practice. It's frowned upon, obviously. The CPA would contact your tax preparer—*me*—as a matter of course during the audit, and I'd have to tell them that you'd fired me. Besides, the bank already knows I was hired to perform the audit. If you turn in an opinion signed by another CPA, they'll question why."

Sharon's eyes narrowed. "How does the bank know we hired you to do the audit? I never told them we planned to engage your services."

"I ran into one of the bank's V.P.'s at the Cowboy Coffee Shop a few days back. It came up in conversation."

Her frown deepened and her eyes narrowed even further, mere slits now. "I don't appreciate you talking about my private business matters in a public place."

At least we were even. I didn't appreciate what she was insinuating, that I had used poor judgment. Besides, it was Kathleen, the bank manager, who'd raised the subject of the loan at the coffee shop, not me. I didn't want to throw Kathleen under the bus, but I didn't want to be blamed for something that wasn't my fault, either. "I wasn't the one who brought it up, and I didn't share any details about your business other than the fact that I'd be performing the audit. The bank would have assumed as much anyway, because they'll know I did your tax work. They'll review copies of the pawn shop's tax returns and your personal tax returns during the underwriting process, and they'll see my name listed on the returns as the preparer. It's standard practice for businesses to use the same CPA for both tax and audit purposes because they're already familiar with the financial records and can perform an audit more efficiently and save fees. In fact, if you hadn't hired me, they'd wonder why."

She didn't look entirely convinced, but she let the matter drop. "Tell you what. There's a couple of items I need to knock off my to-do list this afternoon but, as soon as I do, I'll call Big D Gun Depot myself and demand they get in touch with you immediately. With as much money as we've sent their way, that should light a fire under them. They won't want to risk losing us as a customer."

She had a point. The company was likely to be more responsive to a repeat customer than to me, who they didn't know from Adam. "That's a good idea, Sharon." *Phew.* I was glad we'd worked out a solution. "I'll let you know once I hear from them."

We both stood and she walked me the door. "Take care, Debbie."

"You, too, Sharon. I'll be back in touch soon."

CHAPTER 5
SOMETIMES, NUMBERS DO LIE

FINALLY, I received a call from Big D Gun Depot … *or did I?*

Early Wednesday afternoon, a self-proclaimed "free spirited modern-day poet" popped up on the dating app. He had shaggy hair, a scraggly beard, and an abundance of armpit hair sticking out of his tank top. Clearly, he was looking for a sugar mama to keep him in cannabis and Birkenstocks. *It's not going to be me, buddy.* Just after I swiped left, the office phone rang. Ari had attended her morning classes and come in to work an afternoon shift. She answered the call in her usual upbeat demeanor. "Good afternoon! Debra Ott's office. How may I help you?" She was silent for a few seconds as she listened. "Let me put you on hold for just a moment and see if she's available to take your call." She jabbed the hold button and leaned over in her chair so she could see me. "You want to take a call from Big D Gun Depot?"

Did I ever! "Put them through. Thanks, Ari."

A moment later, the caller's number popped up on my telephone screen. The number began with a 214 area code. The 214 area code covered Dallas and surrounding areas, along with the 469 and 972 area codes that were later added as the population and demand for phone numbers expanded.

However, it was not the same 214 number from the business card Sharon had texted to me earlier. I pushed the button to accept the transfer. "This is Debra Ott."

"Hello, Miss Ott," came a man's voice with a thick Texas drawl. "We heard from our customer Tumbleweed Pawn and Pistols that you need some sort of information from us."

"That's correct." I explained that I was performing an audit and needed to verify the amount due from them to Big D.

"I can tell you right now," he said. "It's eighteen-thousand three-hundred sixty-five dollars and seventy-four cents."

That amount matched the information in my records. *Good.* "I'll need something in writing from you for the file."

"No problem," he said. "I can shoot you an e-mail."

"That would be helpful." Given that I'd found little to verify the company's existence, I wouldn't be satisfied with a mere e-mail, though. "I'll also need to send you a verification by mail. What's your address?" I held my pen at the ready over my sticky note pad.

"Forty-eight forty-eight Lemmon Avenue in Dallas. Suite one-hundred. The zip code is seven five two one nine."

I jotted the address down and then typed it into my browser. Per the links returned, the address belonged to a UPS store that provided private post office box services. My spine tingled. *Something strange is going on.* Even though I was on the phone with a purported representative of Big D, it still felt as if they were attempting to hide from me. Tilting my head to hold the receiver firmly against my shoulder, I grabbed my cell phone and snapped a photo of the number showing on my landline's caller-ID screen. "And what's your physical address?"

"I just gave it to you."

"No," I said. "That address is for a UPS store. I understand you might receive mail there, but I also need the physical address where you run your gun operation."

"But we don't get mail there."

Was it my imagination, or had he lost some of his drawl? "I won't send mail to your physical address," I said. "I just need to note it in my file."

"Hold on a second." There was a rustling sound as the caller covered the receiver with his hand and engaged in a whispered conversation too quiet for me to hear. When he came back on the line, he said, "We don't have a physical location per se. We keep our inventory in storage. Our staff works remotely."

"The address of the storage site will be sufficient."

There was more rustling. I had a sense that he had me on speaker. The usual etiquette was to inform someone who else was present for a call, but he hadn't done so. Yet another odd fact to add to an increasingly long list of strange things with this vendor.

He said, "We generally don't reveal where we store our guns. There's too much chance someone might find out and break into the place. Guns are one of the most targeted items for thieves, you know."

My frustration level had reached its peak. "I will keep the address under wraps, but I have to document it in my files."

"Why?" he asked. "Who's going to see it?"

"Nobody, probably," I said. "But I have professional standards that I have to comply with."

There was another long pause before he rattled off another address. I jotted this one down, too, and also ran it through my browser. The address corresponded to a climate-controlled storage facility in west Dallas. "Unit number?" I asked.

"I'm not sure," he said. "I'd have to check."

"Please do," I said. "I'm happy to hold."

The phone went silent for a few beats, and he returned to the line. "Two thirty-three," he said, not only having lost the drawl but sounding vaguely familiar now.

"Thank you very much," I said. "I think I've got everything I need. Except your name and title, of course."

"My name?"

"Yes," I said. "You didn't mention it."

"Oh," he said. "Sorry about that. I'm … Gordon. Gordon Mingus."

"Gordon Mingus," I repeated as I wrote it down. *Why does that name sound vaguely familiar?* I couldn't quite place it. "And your title?"

A beat or two passed before he said, "I'm the C.F.O. That stands for Chief Financial Officer."

Any accountant would know what CFO stood for. The clarification was unnecessary. *Hmm.* "Got it. Thanks."

When he spoke again, he sounded relieved. "Just give me a call back if you need anything else."

"Will do. Thank you, Gordon."

After we ended the call, I directed Ari to prepare a new letter using the mailing address the man had given me. Then I sat back in my chair to think.

As an auditor, I was expected to exercise a certain degree of professional skepticism, and to use my judgment in determining whether a response was reliable. Although I'd purportedly just spoken with Big D's chief financial officer, every cell in my body squirmed in discomfort.

I turned back to my computer. The screen still displayed a link for the storage facility. I picked up my phone and dialed the number. When a clerk answered my call, I offered a fib. "Hi. I've got a storage unit there, and I can't remember if I've paid my bill for this month. Could you check? It's unit number two-thirty-three."

His fingers clickety-clicked on his keyboard for a few seconds before he said, "Judy Knowles?"

"Yes, that's me." *Liar, liar, Pants on fire.*

"You're all paid up, Ms. Knowles. We received your last payment of fifty-nine dollars on the third of the month."

"And that's for my unit number two-thirty-three?" I asked.

"Yes."

"Could you remind me what size that unit is?"

"Five by five."

"That's small," I said, thinking aloud. How could an extensive gun inventory be stored in such a small unit?

"Would you like to upgrade to a larger size?"

"Not now, but thanks for asking." I bade the man goodbye and sat back in my chair, stunned and befuddled.

What the hell is going on?

CHAPTER 6
OFFICER SEXYPANTS

I STARED AT THE WALL, trying to make sense of the situation. Who had called me from Dallas only a moment before? Was it really someone named Gordon Mingus? Had he lied to me about the unit number, or simply made a mistake? Could Judy Knowles be associated with Big D Gun Depot, maybe an owner of the business? If so, maybe she'd rented the unit under her personal name rather than the name of her gun business so that nobody would know she was storing guns in the unit.

Ari walked into my office with the revised confirmation letter to Big D Gun Depot for me to sign. As I handed it back to her, she eyed me. "You okay, Deb?"

I debated telling her about my professional quandary, but decided against it. Not that I thought she'd blab and word would get back to the Stocktons that I thought one of their vendors seemed sketchy. The reason I didn't want to say anything was because I feared I might be wrong and end up looking foolish. After all, a lot of people worked remotely these days. And was it really so unreasonable for a gun dealer to want to keep the location of their inventory under wraps? Maybe not. Maybe I was only feeling suspicious because finding Allen wriggling and writhing atop another woman only a few days earlier had made me distrustful. I needed some time to think things through. I'd sleep on it and see if things seemed more clear tomorrow.

———

Wednesday was my son-in-law's poker night with his buddies, so my daughter met me for dinner at Tookie's Diner. We'd been going to Tookie's since she was a baby, sitting in a high chair and smearing blueberry pie all over her face. I remembered her years later, sounding out the words on the menu when she was in kindergarten and learning to read, remembered when she had her thirteenth birthday and insisted she was too old to order from the children's menu even though Tookie's had very lax enforcement of the age requirement. I'd once seen an octogenarian order the peanut butter and jelly sandwich from the kid's menu and the waitress hadn't batted an eye. Tonight, though, we both went for the veggie plate. I could never get enough of Tookie's fried okra.

"How's everything with you?" I asked Hayleigh.

"Good," she said. "Work has been busy."

I wasn't surprised. She worked as a nurse for a local pediatric practice. Now that winter was over and the weather was nice, kids had started playing outside again. Sports, skateboards, and bicycles meant broken bones, scrapes, and cuts needing stitches or butterfly bandages.

"How's your father?" I asked, playing nice. For all I cared, he could be covered in oozing boils, but I didn't want to put my daughter in the middle of our marital woes.

"He's lonely," she said.

"Lonely? What about his girlfriend?" I'd assumed he'd had some type of relationship with the woman he'd been having sex with in his office.

"She ended things. I think getting caught made her feel ashamed."

Heh. It was a small consolation to know that while Allen might have had his cake, he was no longer getting to eat her.

Hayleigh speared a cherry tomato and held it aloft. "Dad feels ashamed, too. He knows I'm disgusted with him. He apologized for tearing the family apart. He had tears in his eyes when he said it, too."

I was glad he'd apologized to her but, really, it was the least he could do.

She eyed me closely. "What about you? When are you going to get back on the horse?"

"I'm on a dating app," I said. "Problem is, there's very slim pickings in Tumbleweed."

"Expand your radius," she suggested.

"I already did. I'm at a hundred miles. I'm not going to drive more than two hours to meet someone. I'm barely interested in dating as it is. What I really need is a long-haul trucker who comes through town once a month and takes me to dinner and a movie. That would be perfect."

Hayleigh chuckled. "How'd the home inspection go?"

"Good," I said. "No major problems. Pretty soon, you and I won't just be mother and daughter, we'll be neighbors, too."

"Good," Hayleigh said, and she truly seemed to mean it. It was nice when your children grew up and actually wanted you close instead of trying to distance themselves.

"Whenever you decide to have children, I'll be just around the corner. I can come over and babysit any time."

She rolled her eyes, but grinned. "Mom. Chill. We'll give you a grandbaby when we're good and ready."

When we finished eating, I walked her out to her car in the parking lot and gave her a hug and a kiss on the check. "I love you, Haystack."

"Love you, too, Mom."

———

I was asleep in my studio apartment at 3:18 am when movement woke me. Buddha, who'd been curled up next to me only a moment before, now stood on the bed. He stared toward the door, his ears pricked. I heard something then, too. A muffled thump came from the stairwell.

What the …?

I threw the covers back and went to the apartment door. When I heard nothing for a moment or two, I turned the deadbolt. The click as it slid open sounded loud in the quiet space. I pulled the door open only an inch or two and looked down the dimly lit stairway. Nobody and nothing were there. Not a person. Not a rat. Not even a spider or errant cockroach as far as I could tell. *What had made that thump?* Maybe someone had drank too much at the local bar, and bumped into the ground level door on their way down the sidewalk. But no, that couldn't be it. The bar had closed hours ago. Could a gust of wind have blown something up against the door?

I wasn't left to wonder long. Another *thump* came from down below, followed by a *crack* as the door that led from the stairwell to the sidewalk separated from the frame and titled on its hinges. *Someone is prying the door open!*

In a split second, I closed the door and slid the deadbolt home. The studio had no landline, and my cell phone was in my purse. I grabbed my purse from the table. Realizing that I'd be a sitting duck in my studio, and not wanting to leave my precious cat behind, I slung my purse over my shoulder and scooped Buddha up in my arms, clutching him to my chest in a death grip. I dashed to the back window, planning to flee down the fire escape and phone the police once I was safely out of my apartment. But when I looked out and saw a dark shadow coming up the fire escape, I realized fleeing was no longer an option. Panic sent my brains scrambling and wrapped its fingers tight around my throat. *I'm trapped!*

Or am I?

I scurried over and yanked on the rope for the pulldown attic. Still clutching Buddha in one arm, I used my free hand to pull myself up the ladder. As soon as I was in the attic, I set my cat and purse aside and reached down to pull the ladder back up. Once the hatch closed, I yanked on the rope to pull it up through the small hole until the knot on the underside hit the wood of the ceiling. I quickly tied the rope around a beam so that it would be difficult for anyone to pull it back down from below to open the attic.

Another thump and crack sounded as I dug through my purse for my phone. Whoever had pried open the door below was now in my apartment. *Who is it? And why are they here?*

The sound of footsteps came from my apartment below me. My hands shook as I dialed 9-1-1 and turned down the volume on my phone so that whoever was in my apartment wouldn't be able to hear the dispatcher.

"Nine-one-one," came the dispatcher's voice, barely audible at the low volume setting. "What's your emergency?"

I whispered. "Someone just broke into my apartment! I'm hiding in my attic!"

"What's your address?"

I whispered my address.

"Stay on the line," the woman said. "We've got officers en route."

I crouched in the small space, quivering with fear. I heard a window being opened in my studio below, followed by two male voices.

"There's no sign of her. No purse, either."

"She's not here, then. Women don't go anywhere without their purses."

The faint *woo-woo-woo* of a siren sounded in the distance.

A nice thing about living in a small town was that, no matter where you were, the police station wasn't far away.

"It's the cops!" said the first man. "Let's get the fuck out of here!"

There was a scrambling sound, and then the sound of footsteps banging down the metal stairs of the fire escape. A few seconds later, more footsteps sounded, these stampeding up the wooden steps of the stairwell. A different male voice came from my studio below, a deep, booming voice. "Tumble-weed Police!" called the officer. "Come out with your hands up!"

I heard fast footwork, then a second male voice. "Nobody's here. Looks like they went out the back window."

Over the phone line came the dispatcher's voice. "Officers have arrived at your residence."

"I hear them," I said. "Do they know I'm in the attic?" The last thing I wanted to do was surprise them and accidentally get shot.

"They've been informed," she assured me. "You take care now."

"Thanks."

As I slid the phone back into my purse, the first cop called, "It's safe to come out of the attic now! Slow and easy, please!"

I untied the rope from the beam and used my foot to push the hatch open. I peered down through the open hole to see an attractive man looking back up at me. He was older than your average police officer, around my age, with silver and dark hair like a wolf. He was tall and fit, with strong, broad shoulders. The badge on his vest read D. Mooney.

He held his gun at the ready, down at his side, as he looked up at me. "Is it just you up there?"

"Me and my cat," I replied.

He slid his gun into his holster, grabbed the bottom rung of the ladder, and pulled it down into place. Buddha walked over and peered down at the man, too. "He friendly?" the cop asked.

"Yes," I replied. "He's too lazy to be mean."

A second cop stepped into view. I recognized this officer as Sergeant Roscoe Starr. He had sandy hair, a little scruff, and a nice smile. He'd been a couple years ahead of Hayleigh in school, and quite popular. I'd served on the PTA with his mother years ago.

Starr waved up at me. "Hi, Mrs. Ott."

"Hi, Roscoe."

He gestured toward the back of my apartment. "Looks like the prowlers went out your back window. Any idea what kind of car they're driving?"

I shook my head. "Not a clue."

He turned to Mooney. "I'll cruise the streets, see what I can find."

Mooney gave him a nod. Roscoe headed off and Mooney looked back up at me and Buddha. "Hand me that lazy cat."

I retrieved Buddha and held him out to the man. Mooney took him from me, and bounced him slightly in his arms. "I'd guess I'm holding at least fifteen pounds here. You need to put this fat fella on a diet." He set Buddha on the floor in my studio. Buddha cast him a look of disgust, as if he knew the officer had made fun of his pussycat paunch. He sauntered off, his tail swishing. After walking a few steps, he plunked himself down in the middle of the floor and licked his empty nut sack, as chill as ever.

Mooney held out a hand to help me down, too. I was embarrassed for such an attractive man to see me in my short cotton nightgown, especially since it bore a cartoon image of books along with the words I'M BOOKED TONIGHT. Smart, sure. But sexy? Not in the least.

He eyed my nightie, then cast a glance at the towering pile of mystery novels on my night table. "A reader, huh? No wonder you were smart enough to outwit the intruders, Mrs. Ott."

"Call me Debbie," I said. "And it's not Mrs. anymore. At least, it won't be in a few weeks."

He cast another glance at my stack of mysteries. "Planning to murder your husband?"

"No," I said. "Not that he doesn't deserve it."

He arched a brow, but didn't ask me to elaborate. He held out a hand, inviting me to take a seat at the bistro set. Once I'd sat down, he dropped into the seat across from me and whipped a notepad and pen from the chest pocket of his uniform. "Tell me what happened."

I gave him the rundown. Buddha waking me from sleep —*thank goodness*. Someone forcing the front door open downstairs. My attempt to flee via the fire escape, but noting another man coming up the steps. "And then I realized the only place I could hide where they wouldn't find me was in the attic. So, I grabbed my cat and up we went."

"Any idea who they were?"

"None."

"So, you didn't recognize their voices?"

I shook my head.

He glanced around. "Do you keep anything valuable in here? Jewelry, maybe?"

"No," I said. "I've never been one for expensive jewelry, and anything else of value is back at my house—I mean, my husband's house—I mean my ex-husband's house—I mean my soon-to-be-ex-husband's house." I rolled my eyes. "Sheesh. I must sound like an idiot, huh?"

He gave me a soft smile. "Not at all. I'm divorced myself. I've been where you are. It's a strange time when you're estranged, waiting for things to become official. Like being in marital limbo."

I exhaled, glad to feel understood. "I heard one of the

intruders note that my purse was missing. I'd taken it up into the attic with me."

Mooney raised his brows. "Your purse? Maybe they were after your wallet or car keys. That's your Lexus outside, right?"

"Yes."

"It's a nice car." He looked up, as if thinking out loud. "Still, car thefts are rare these days. With all the security on cars, it's much harder to steal them and much easier to locate stolen vehicles." He eyed me. "Any reason why someone might have come after you personally?"

"You mean, they might have been here to hurt me rather than rob me?"

He raised his palms. "Just trying to consider all the possibilities."

I shook my head. "I can't imagine why anyone would want to do me harm. I don't consort with dangerous types. I'm an accountant. I run the CPA firm downstairs. I live a pretty boring life." I cringed as soon as the word *boring* left my mouth. This cop was attractive as hell and here I was, selling myself short. "Well, maybe boring isn't exactly the right word. But I don't engage in risky behavior or run around with criminals."

A grin played about his mouth. "Not the naughty type, then?"

I crossed my arms over my chest, remembering then that not only was I wearing a short nightgown, but my girls were hanging free. A grin tugged at my lips, too. "I'm only naughty when the occasion calls for it."

"You being a CPA might explain things," he said. "Most criminals aren't too smart. They might think that since you run an accounting firm you keep a lot of cash on hand."

I felt my shoulders relax a bit. I was relieved we had a theory to go on.

He cocked his head. "Any chance your husband could be

behind this? Maybe trying to get out of giving you your share of the property in your divorce?"

At the thought of Allen hiring hit men to do away with me, I barked a laugh. "No. No way. Allen's been fair, and he's never been the abusive or vindictive type."

"All right, then." He gestured to the door, which was splintered. "Both of your doors will need to be replaced. Got somewhere safe you can go tonight?"

I debated what to do. I could go to Hayleigh's house and sleep in her guest room, but I hated to wake her up this late. And on the off chance that whoever had come to my apartment was after me instead of valuables to steal, I didn't want to lead them to her doorstep. "I suppose I could stay with my husband, or check into a hotel."

"Tell you what," Officer Mooney said. "I've got a converted garage that I rent out on AirBnB. Nobody's staying there for the next few days. It's yours if you want it. Free of charge."

"Really? That's so kind and generous." I had to fight not to swoon.

He lifted one shoulder, nonchalant. "You'll be safe there. Can't have you getting robbed or killed. It would make the department look bad." He gave me a teasing smile. He jotted the address and the entry code on his notepad, then ripped off the sheet and handed it to me. "I might need to hire you come tax time next year. I just relocated to Tumbleweed from Fort Worth a few weeks back. I was a detective there, but I was ready for something a little slower paced. Want to enjoy my life while I still can, and the mountains of New Mexico and Colorado are an easy drive from here."

"You like to hike?"

"As often as I can," he said. "You?"

"Same. I take a lot of road trips to state and national parks. Offsets being cooped up in an office all week sitting on my butt."

Turning back to more immediate matters, he said, "I hope you can get a decent night's sleep. I'm going to stick around here, see if I can lift some prints or find any other evidence."

"Thanks."

I grabbed a pair of yoga pants and a bra, and slipped them on in my tiny bathroom. While he dusted the doorframe and knob, I rounded up some essentials and quickly packed a suitcase. I slid Buddha into his carrier, too.

"Let me carry the beefy boy for you," Mooney said. "I need the exercise."

He picked up Buddha's carrier and followed me down the stairs, reaching out a gloved hand to push the exterior door open for me. After helping me load my things in my car, he raised a hand in goodbye. "I'll let you know if we find any clues."

"Thanks, Officer Mooney."

"Call me Daniel."

My heart fluttered like a butterfly in my chest. "Okay. Thanks, Daniel."

CHAPTER 7
WHEN A STRANGER CALLS

DANIEL'S converted garage was outfitted with all the latest security gadgets. Motion-activated exterior lights. A Ring doorbell with a video camera. An alarm system. I suppose it was to be expected, with him being a cop and all. The space was sparsely furnished, but decorated much nicer than my studio apartment. The king-sized bed sported an amazingly comfortable memory-foam mattress, but given how much adrenaline was working its way out of my system I nevertheless had a hard time sleeping. Hiding in my attic earlier, scared stiff that the intruders would find me and hurt me, had taken not just an emotional toll, but also a physical one. My muscles ached from being tensed so hard for those terrifying minutes until the police arrived. My thoughts were still a jumbled mess when I woke Thursday morning—if you could even call it waking. It was more like I came to the realization that it was time for me to get ready for work.

After a cup of coffee at the kitchenette, I cleaned myself up, dressed, and carried Buddha out to my car at the curb. Daniel's Tumbleweed PD cruiser sat in his driveway. After working the graveyard shift last night, he was probably sleeping now. He'd seen me in my sleepwear. I wondered what his pajamas looked like ... or whether he wore any.

I drove to the office and pulled into my reserved parking spot to see yellow cordon tape forming an X over the door to my studio apartment. No doubt other Tumbleweeders had seen it, too. Good thing only a handful of people knew I had moved into the apartment. Otherwise, my phone would be ringing all day long with nosy questions.

In an abundance of caution, I locked my office door behind me. The first thing I did after releasing Buddha from his carrier and sitting down at my desk was to read over the applicable Generally Accepted Auditing Standards to see if they could provide any further guidance about what to do about the audit. They didn't. They told me what I already knew, which was that I had to approach my audit work with a reasonable level of professional skepticism. I read over the code of professional conduct on the website for the Texas State Board of Public Accountancy. It didn't help, either. The reality was that I wouldn't feel comfortable issuing an unqualified opinion on the financial statements for Tumbleweed Pawn & Pistols unless I could obtain greater assurance that Big D Gun Depot was a legitimate business. I supposed I'd wait to make a final decision once the confirmation letter was signed and returned.

Arielle arrived later that morning, after an early class. As she came in the door, she gestured toward the yellow tape down the walk. "Why is there crime scene tape on your apartment?"

"Someone broke into my place last night."

Her eyes popped wide and her mouth gaped. "What?!"

I gave her the details. "I have no idea who it was other than it was two men. The police were going to dust for prints. Sergeant Starr drove around looking for them, but as far as I know he didn't see anyone suspicious."

She shuddered. "I hope they find the guys. It's creepy to

think of strangers lurking around, especially since we don't know what they were after."

"That's why we're going to keep this door locked from now on." I walked over and locked the deadbolt on the glass door.

Just after lunchtime, Arielle answered an incoming call. I was immersed in a monthly review of financial statements for a local donut shop, but looked up when she walked into my office.

"Some guy is on the phone," she said. "He wants to talk to you."

"Who is it?"

"He won't tell me," she said. "He says it's personal."

"What phone number is he calling from?" I asked, hoping I'd recognize it.

"The caller ID readout just says 'Unknown.'"

Having gotten little sleep, I was already on edge, and I felt my ire rise further. "It's probably a salesperson." The 'it's personal' ploy was likely the man's way of trying to get past my gatekeeper. "Go ahead and transfer the call." If it was a telemarketer, I'd give them a piece of my mind. A few choice words, too.

Ari returned to her desk and transferred the call to me. My caller ID readout also showed 'Unknown.' I picked up the receiver. "This is Debra Ott."

A man's voice came over the line. It sounded strange and robotic, as if he were using a voice changing app. "Resign from the audit."

Resign from the audit? I had three audits in various stages of progress, though my audit of Tumbleweed Pawn and Pistols was by far the biggest project. It was also the only one in which I'd run into any problems. Nevertheless, I asked for clarification. "I'm working on several audits. Which one are you referring to?"

"The pawn shop."

I'd figured as much. All of the others had gone smoothly. An eerie sense slithered up my spin. "Why should I resign?"

"Because I told you to."

If the guy was going to threaten me, he could at least identify himself. "And you are …?"

I waited for the man to fill in the blank. When he did, it was with, "None of your business."

Who the hell is this guy? "The owners of the pawn shop hired me. Only they can fire me. I have a contract to provide services and I'm not going to breach it. It's my legal and ethical obligation to finish the job. I'm certainly not going to resign because some stranger tells me to."

"Resign now," he demanded again before upping the ante with, "or you'll wish you had. And keep your mouth shut if you know what's good for you." With that, he hung up.

I sat back in my seat, shocked, scared, baffled, and bewildered. Nothing like this had ever happened to me before. Accounting was generally a safe and relatively humdrum profession. Now, here I was getting threats! And from an unknown person at that. It was all so weird.

I didn't know who had called me or why, but I did know one thing for certain. There was no way in hell I'd resign from the audit now. Something very strange was going on, and I was going to get to the bottom of it.

CHAPTER 8
ETCH AND SKETCH

WHEN I HUNG UP, Ari came to my office door. "Who was it? A salesman?"

I shook my head. "It was someone who wants us off the pawn shop audit."

"Why?"

"I don't know. They told me to resign or I'd be sorry."

Ari winced. "Things are getting weird around here."

"They most certainly are."

As Ari returned to her desk, I retrieved my purse and pulled out the business card Daniel Mooney had given me the night before. Though I didn't want to wake him, I figured I should fill him in on this latest development. I dialed the number. It rang five times before a gravelly voice answered. "Officer Mooney."

"Sorry to wake you," I said. "This is Debbie Ott."

He cleared his throat. "Good morning, Debbie. How can I help you?"

"Someone just called my office. I'm in the middle of auditing the Tumbleweed Pawn & Pistols. The caller told me to resign from the audit."

"Have you mentioned the call to anyone else?"

"Only my assistant, Arielle."

A rustling noise came through the phone, as if he was on the move. "I'm on my way. Don't tell anyone else."

"Not even the owners of the pawn shop?"

"Especially not the owners of the pawn shop."

After we ended the call, I stood and walked to Ari's desk. "I called the cop who's investigating the break-in. He said we need to keep mum about the call that came in a few minutes ago."

She mimed locking her lips and tossing the key, though she then immediately reopened her mouth to pepper me with questions. "Does he think the call and the break-in are related? Is he going to try to trace the call? Are we in danger?"

Unfortunately, I had no answers for her, and I had the same questions myself.

Officer Mooney arrived a few minutes later, and gestured for me to follow him back to my office. He closed the door and had me repeat what the caller had said on the phone. He ran a hand over his head. "We're still waiting on the lab to run the prints I lifted from your doors last night. It could take a few days. The T-Weed police department is sorely underfunded."

"That doesn't surprise me in the least." People complained to me about how much they had to pay in income taxes, and I knew they complained about the sales and property taxes that funded the city governments, too. Nobody wanted to foot the bill for a fully-funded department.

He pointed to my small conference table. "Can we sit?"

"Of course."

He took a seat at one end of the table, and I slid into the chair next to him, swiveling it to face him. He whipped out his notepad and said, "Tell me about the audit."

"Most of the audit has turned out as expected," I said.

"Sharon keeps accurate books. There's been just one big problem. One of their gun vendors has failed to confirm their account figures. I can't seem to track them down to any legitimate address." I told him about the returned letter, my visit to Sharon Stockton, the odd phone call from the man who'd given me the mailing address for the UPS store and the phony storage unit number. "He said his name was Gordon Mingus."

Daniel's brows pulled together. "Gordon Mingus?"

"Yes. Does that name mean something to you?"

"Gordon and Mingus are both towns between here and Dallas, but as a person's name? No."

I showed him the photo I'd taken of my landline's caller-ID screen, the one that showed the incoming call from the 214 area code, the call that purportedly came from Gordon Mingus. He took my phone from my hand and forwarded the pic to his own phone before returning my phone to me.

When I finished filling him in, I asked, "What now?"

"I'm going to see what I can find out about this phone number, and I'm going over to the pawn shop."

"Are you going to tell them about the call I got today?"

"No," he said. "I'm going to act like I'm just there about the break-in, to see if someone might have pawned your property."

"But nothing was taken."

"The Stocktons don't know that," he said. "Or at least they shouldn't. While I'm there, I'm going to take a look at their gun inventory, see if there's anything suspicious about it. In the meantime, you keep your door locked. If you see anything that gives you pause, don't hesitate to call it in. Hear me?"

I gave him a salute. "Yes, sir!"

That roguish grin played about his lips again. "I'll be in touch."

I could hardly wait.

———

On Thursday evening, a *rap-rap-rap* came at the door of Officer Mooney's converted garage. I looked out the peephole to see him standing there with a shaggy mutt at his knee. I opened the door.

"Got some news for you," he said. "A gift, too."

"A gift? What for?"

"Just something to cheer you up. I know you've been under a lot of stress. May we come in?"

"Of course." I stepped back and held out a hand to invite him and his dog inside. I noticed that he wore a holster on both hips today, not just his right hip as usual. Wearing the two holsters made him look like a wild west gunslinger ready to duel in the dusty streets of old El Paso. Buddha sauntered over to give the dog a sniff. The dog wagged his tail and sniffed Buddha right back. I bent over and stroked the dog's neck. "Who do we have here?"

"That's Zigzag," Daniel said. "He's part border collie. You wouldn't know it to look at him now, but he was full of energy when he was a pup. Used to zigzag all over the yard."

I gave the dog one last pat and straightened. "Can I get you a Coke, Daniel? Maybe some tea?"

"Got anything stronger?" he asked. "I might still be in uniform, but my shift is over."

I opened a kitchen cabinet and pulled out a bottle of bourbon I'd bought at the liquor store after work. I figured it would help calm my nerves and enable me to sleep tonight. "How would you like it?"

"Neat. Three fingers."

I retrieved two lowball glasses. I filled his glass twice as full as mine. I wanted to relax, not get rip-roaring drunk. Clearly, he could handle his liquor better than I could.

I handed him his glass and he raised it. "Cheers."

I clinked my glass against his in toast and we sipped the

bourbon. As I drank, Daniel gave me a look that ignited the same slow burn in my nether regions that the bourbon had ignited in my throat.

"First things first." I cocked my head. "You mentioned a gift?"

He reached into his pants pocket and pulled out a pair of dangle earrings in a rounded diamond shape. They were made of cheap white plastic and weren't all that pretty, to be honest. But I wasn't about to look a gift horse in the mouth. Daniel earned a modest public servant's salary, and most men knew squat about women's accessories. *It's the thought that counts, right?*

"Thanks!" I said, with forced enthusiasm. "They'll go perfect with my suits. White will match any of them."

He led me over to the sofa and took a seat on one end, angling himself so that he could address me directly as I sat down on the other end. "The lab didn't get any hits on the fingerprints that were on the door frame or knob at your studio apartment. That means that either the guys who broke into your place aren't in the system, or they wore gloves and didn't leave prints."

"Darn." I hoped they'd be able to identify the men and make a quick arrest.

"That phone with the two one four area code? It's a prepaid burner, not registered to anyone."

Untraceable, in other words.

He continued. "When I went to the pawn shop, I asked for records on all items pawned since your place was broken into. Warren Stockton asked me what I needed the information for. I told them your home had been burgled and that I was looking for stolen jewelry the robber might have pawned. Warren expressed concern and condolences, and asked if there was anything in particular he should keep an eye out for."

Hmm. "Seems like exactly what you'd expect an innocent party to say."

"That's what I thought, too. But it's not what he said that has me wondering. It was the look he gave his son Ruger."

"What look?"

Daniel mimicked Warren, looking at me sideways with squinty eyes and lips pressed hard together.

I wasn't quite sure how to take it. "You think they realized you were lying to them?"

"Maybe," Daniel said, "or maybe they thought you lied to me, that you wrongfully reported that jewelry had been taken during the burglary so you could file an insurance claim. Hard to say. At any rate, after looking through the records, I nosed around in the guns. I told them I was a gun nut and had quite a collection, and that I was looking to add to it. I had Ruger show me dozens of guns until I found what I was looking for."

"Which was …?"

He pulled a small pistol from his left holster.

I raised my palms and leaned back.

He arched his brows. "It's not loaded."

"I don't care. Guns scare me."

"Glad to hear it," he said, his face serious. "They should." He lay the gun down on the sofa between us, pointing away. He ran a finger over a line of numbers and letters engraved in the metal. "See this serial number here? That number identifies this specific gun. Federal law requires the serial number be engraved at least point zero zero three inches deep. That's enough depth to keep the digits from wearing off under normal usage. Gun thieves will often file off the serial numbers to make the guns untraceable."

I bobbed my head to let him know I was following. "So, a gun without a serial number is a big red flag?"

"Exactly. It means it's been stolen. It's standard procedure for pawn shops to run a gun's serial number through the online databases to make sure they aren't buying stolen property."

"This particular gun isn't stolen then, since it still has the serial number on it?"

"Look closer," he said. "See anything unusual?"

I leaned over and looked at the gun. "It looks very clean and shiny." I shrugged. "That's all I notice."

He pointed to a barely perceptible line along the metal frame next to the serial number. "See this? Looks to me like someone might have added a layer of metal here."

I leaned in closer and squinted. It took a moment of intense concentration, but then I saw the line he was referring to. The metal was ever so slightly darker to the left, and lighter under the serial number. I sat back up. "Why would they do that?"

"So they could put a new serial number on the gun, a legitimate serial number from another gun of this particular make and model, a twin, if you will. Hell, for all I know, there could be dozens of pistols just like this etched with that same serial number." He went on to give me a lesson in metal. "Metal is formed of crystallized grains that fit together like a three-dimensional puzzle. The etching process changes the metal underneath the etching, it damages the underlying metal much in the way that the legs of heavy furniture leave the carpet underneath it changed and compacted." He said that law enforcement traditionally used an acid-etching technique to try to recover old serial numbers that had been filed away. It was a difficult process with mixed results. "But there's a new technique, a high-tech one called Electron Backscatter Diffraction, or EBSD for short. Scientists can use an electron microscope to examine the damage to the underlying atoms. They can tell where the crystals underneath the missing serial number have been impacted by a die tool or heated by a laser. With this technique, they can recreate serial numbers that have been fully filed away."

"Wow," I said. "That sounds so futuristic."

"I've got a buddy with the Bureau of Alcohol, Tobacco, and Firearms field office in Fort Worth. He's going to see if he can get their lab to run a test on this gun for me. They might refuse. They're busy and have their own cases to handle, but it's worth a shot."

A grin played about my mouth. "Worth a shot?"

He grinned right back. "That pun was unintentional. Anyway, I have the day off tomorrow. My buddy suggested I drive to Fort Worth and pay him a visit in person. He said the lab will have a harder time saying 'no' directly to my face. I'll have dinner with my kids, then spend the night at my son's place. I'll come back to Tumbleweed on Saturday."

I reached over and took his hand in mine, giving it a squeeze. "Thanks for going the extra mile for me."

"Extra mile?" He chuckled. "Now who's making lame puns?"

We shared a laugh.

I pondered the situation. "I wonder if the Stocktons purchased that gun from Big D Gun Depot."

"It's possible," Daniel said.

I mulled some more. "Assuming the gun came from Big D and it is, in fact, stolen, the question remains whether the Stocktons were aware of the situation. They could have been duped." The Stocktons were a well-established Tumbleweed family, well-respected and well-liked, too. Despite my recent minor head-butting with Sharon, I harbored no ill will. I was a businesswoman, too, and I knew she'd only been doing what she thought was best for the pawn shop. "Other than Ruger Stockton taking bets on who'd win the local beauty pageant, the Stocktons have always been law-abiding as far as I know."

"None of them has a record," Daniel said. "I checked. With any luck, we'll get some answers soon."

Our discussion complete, we relaxed back on the couch

and turned our conversation to more personal matters. I learned that Daniel had a son and a daughter back in Fort Worth, both adults like Hayleigh. He and his ex-wife had split amicably three years earlier. The two had simply grown apart over the years, but not realized just how far until their children left home and they discovered they had little in common anymore. He told me about his time as a detective with the Fort Worth police department, handling mostly drug crimes. He asked about my life, too, and I told him how I'd started off working at a larger accounting firm here in Tumbleweed, but eventually ventured out on my own after tiring of working long hours and weekends to line the partners' pockets rather than my own.

When our small talk ran its course, we found a funny movie on television and watched it together, simply enjoying our bourbon and each other's companionship. *I could get used to this.*

When the movie ended, it was nearly eleven o'clock. I stood. "I'd better get to bed."

He stood, too, his gaze moving to the bed behind us before returning to my face. "I envy those sheets."

Laughing, I put a hand on his chest and pushed. "Go." *Before I pull you out of that uniform and into that bed with me.*

CHAPTER 9
IT'S NOT JUST THE WEASEL THAT GOES POP!

ON FRIDAY MORNING, I slid into a silky white blouse, my light gray pantsuit, and my navy-blue loafers. I accessorized with a scarf in complementary colors and the earrings Daniel had given me. *Lord, those plastic earrings are even uglier on than off.* But I kept them on in the off chance I ran across him on my way to my car. I didn't want to insult the guy. But I did fluff my hair out around my face so that they'd be less visible.

I arrived at the office with Buddha in tow. The cordon tape had been removed from the exterior door of the studio apartment, and a handyman was hanging a new door, a sturdy metal one in a strong frame. If anyone tried to break into that apartment again, they'd have a much harder time.

I entered my office and locked the door behind me. Arielle had an exam this morning and wouldn't be coming in until lunchtime. Until then, it would be just me and my cat. Buddha took his usual seat atop the back of one of the armchairs so that he could bask in the sunlight streaming through the front window. As always, passersby smiled and talked to him through the glass. Some even tapped to see if he'd respond. The Zen kitty would simply stare back at them.

He was too enlightened to be concerned with the things of this earth.

I handled a couple of client meetings that morning. One of them had discovered a stack of receipts for charitable contributions they'd set aside and forgotten about, and needed me to file an amended return to claim the additional deductions. The other had received an inquiry from the Internal Revenue Service regarding a sale of stock she'd inherited. I assured her she owed no tax, and that all we'd need to do was provide the IRS with evidence of the value of the stock at the time it was bequeathed to her.

Buddha and I were in the office alone when Ari arrived shortly after noon with a big smile on her face.

Despite my unease over the threatening phone call, seeing her grin made me smile, too. Smiles are contagious, after all. "I take it the exam went well?"

"Easy as pie." She did a happy dance in the middle of the floor.

"I doubt it was easy," I said. "You're just smart and studied hard."

She groaned. "Ugh. You make me sound like such a dork!"

"If the shoe fits … But speaking of food, how about I order us some lunch to celebrate the A you're sure to get?"

Her face brightened. "Can we order from Golden Dragon?"

"Sure," I said. "Chinese sounds great. We'll get pie from Tookie's for dessert."

We looked over the Golden Dragon's menu online at her desk. Once we'd decided, I tucked my hair behind my ear to call the restaurant to place an order for delivery. They promised to have it to my office in thirty minutes or less. I'd walk over to Tookie's to get our pie after we ate our lunch. Couldn't hurt to stretch my legs.

As I returned the receiver to the cradle, Ari eyed my lobes. "New earrings?"

"Yes. Officer Mooney gave them to me."

She snorted. "He's got awful taste in jewelry, but good taste in women."

"I don't know whether to thank you or fire you."

Ari said, "You'd never fire me. I'm too reliable."

"Damn, you're right again."

I'd just turned to walk back into my office when a soft *pop-pop-pop* met my ears, followed by the *ksssh* of the front window of my office shattering and falling in shards to the floor. A line of holes appeared in the wall that separated my office from the reception area. The line was growing longer and heading right for us.

"Get down!" I tackled Ari as if I were a member of the Dallas Cowboys' defense, taking her and her chair to the ground, out of the line of fire. We shrieked in each other's ears as the bullets hit the wall just above her desk and drywall dust rained down on us. *Pop-pop-pop!*

In what must have been mere seconds but felt like an eternity, the popping sound stopped. Ari and I had survived. *But what about my cat?*

"Buddha!" Tentatively, I raised my head over the back of Ari's desk, frantically searching for him.

My cat was crouched on the floor, his paws splayed and his head down. His eyes were wide and his mouth open, but he bore no blood. Thank God he'd had the sense to get away from the window when the shooting started. I crawled out from behind the desk and grabbed him, cradling him to my chest.

Still cowering behind her desk, Ari whipped out her cell phone and dialed 9-1-1. "We need the police!" she cried. "There's been a drive-by shooting on the square!"

It took only seconds for us to hear the *woo-woo-woo* of a distant siren and a minute for law enforcement to arrive. We were still sitting on the floor, hunkered down below window level where the exterior brick could protect us, when Sergeant Starr arrived. "You two okay?" he called through the shattered window.

"We're fine," I said, though I only meant that we were okay physically. Mentally was a whole 'nother story. We were both in shock. While we'd suffered no physical injuries, I was certain we'd suffer some psychological issues once the horror wore off.

Ari pulled herself up from the floor and into her chair. Her entire body was shaking. She wrapped her arms around herself as if to hold herself together.

Keeping a close eye on the square, Sergeant Starr asked, "Did either of you see what the shooter was driving?"

"No." I hadn't seen the shooter or the car. All I'd seen was my front window turn into a shower of glass shards and the bullets penetrating the wall. Ari hadn't seen the car or shooter either. It had all happened too fast.

He squeezed a button on his shoulder-mounted radio. "Did any of the callers get an ID on the vehicle?"

The dispatchers voice came back. "Several said they thought the shots came from a pickup."

"Did they get a color or a license plate? Even a partial would help."

The dispatcher said, "No plate number. One caller thought the bullets came from a white pickup. Another said it was a dark pickup."

The cop groaned in frustration. "That's no help. There's as many pickups in Tumbleweed as there are pricks on a prickly pear cactus. How many people were in the truck?"

"Some said they only saw a driver. Others said the shooter was in the passenger seat."

Sergeant Starr thanked the dispatcher. Thinking out loud, he said, "Two people would make more sense. The driver could have shot out the passenger window, but he'd have to keep an eye on the road, too. His aim would have been harder to maintain and he'd be more likely to miss."

He turned to look at the holes on my wall, and my gaze followed his. What started as a relatively straight line curved downward and ended in a big hole where several bullets had hit close together. Clearly, the shooter had aimed for me and Ari on the floor. Thank goodness he'd missed us. It probably wasn't easy to shoot at a moving target from a moving vehicle.

I turned to address the officer through the window. "Did they shoot up the whole square?"

"They only fired on your office. Two other businesses were shot up overnight, but they were closed at the time."

Was the situation a random crime spree? Or had yesterday's caller come after me? He said I'd be sorry if I didn't resign from the pawn shop audit. Was this him making good on that threat? If so, had he intended to kill me?

Two other police cruisers careened up out front and officers emerged with their weapons drawn. Starr's eyes roamed the square before he turned back to me. "The courthouse has security cameras. I'll see if they picked up anything." He called out to a female officer. "Keep an eye on this office."

"Yes, sir."

She walked over to stand in front of my office, her gaze repeatedly scanning the area in case the shooters returned. I prayed they wouldn't come back.

Ari began to sob. I didn't blame her one bit. I'd feel like sobbing myself if I weren't so damn angry. Nobody had a right to break into my apartment and nobody had a right to shoot up my office like this. I was beyond pissed.

I called to the officer. "Can my assistant go home?"

The female officer said, "Sure. I'll get her an escort."

In minutes, another officer arrived and helped Ari into his front seat. He loaded her bicycle into the trunk of his cruiser.

Miraculously, the bike had escaped the barrage with only a flat tire.

I reached out and gave Ari a supportive pat on the shoulder. "I'll pay to have that tire replaced. Hell, I'll buy you an entirely new bike if you want." The seventeen dollars an hour I paid her seemed paltry now.

She gazed up at me. "I nearly lost my life. I want a brand-new Mustang."

Her joke told me she was already feeling a bit better.

The delivery driver from Golden Dragon arrived, a bag in his hand. He took one look at the window and said, "Holy shit! What happened?"

"Drive-by," I said.

"Whoa."

He handed me the bag, and I handed him a tip in return. I fished out the containers containing my lunch and handed the bag through the cruiser's open window to Ari. I might be sending her off with PTSD, but at least I was also sending her off with a delicious lunch—assuming her stomach would unknot itself to allow her to eat it.

"You can work remotely for as long as you'd like," I told her. I planned on working remotely for the time being, too. I wouldn't feel safe re-opening the office until whoever did this was caught.

Please, Lord. Let that be very soon!

CHAPTER 10
A GRAVE SITUATION

THE FEMALE OFFICER, Buddha, and I were waiting on an officer to arrive with plywood to board up my windows when Hope McIntyre strolled up the sidewalk. Hope had thick, straight blond hair pulled back in her usual carefree ponytail. She wasn't nearly as thin as her dark-haired, pageant-winning sister, Glory, whose shadow she'd lived in during their childhoods. But she wasn't nearly as shallow as her sister, either. On her head sat a cap with the Tumbleweed Today newspaper logo.

She stopped at the yellow cordon tape that had been tied around the posts out front and looked through the shattered window, greeting me with a tentative smile. "You okay, Mrs. Ott?" she called.

"Luckily, yes."

"Two other places were shot up last night, and I heard your office was hit just a few minutes ago. Do you have anything you'd like to say?"

"Sure," I said. "Aaaaaaah!"

Hope laughed. "How many A's in that?"

"A dozen, at least." My smile faltered on my face. "I don't really know anything to tell you, Hope. I don't know who might have done this. I didn't see anything. It all happened too fast." That wasn't entirely true. My gut told me the drive-by had something to do with Big D Gun Depot. But, without hard evidence, I shouldn't make an accusation that could have repercussions on my client. The Stocktons would appear guilty by association, and could sue me for defamation.

"I understand," she said. "Mind if I take some photos for my article?"

I knew she was only asking as a courtesy. The square was a public place and she had every right to snap a picture. Heck, a huge group of T-Weeders stood on the courthouse lawn behind her, gaping and snapping shots of my office. "Go right ahead," I said.

"Thanks."

As she took photos of my shattered windows, my ringtone blared with an incoming call. I returned to my desk and eyed the screen. It was Officer Mooney calling. No doubt Sergeant Starr or one of the other officers had called him to let him know what happened.

I walked into my office, closed my bullet hole-riddled door, and plopped down in my chair. "Hi, Daniel."

"I heard what happened." His voice was grave and his tone curt. "I'm on my way back to Tumbleweed."

I remembered his plans to have dinner with his children that evening and my heart constricted. "I hate for you to miss dinner with your kids." I knew how much my time with my daughter meant to me, and I didn't want to deprive him of that simple joy.

"I'll get back to Fort Worth for a visit soon," he said.

"Where are you?" I asked.

"On Interstate Twenty. Just past the exit for Gordon, coming up on the exit for Mingus."

In other words, he was about seventy miles east of Fort Worth. Given that the shooting had taken place only an hour before, he was making damn good time. "You must be doing ninety to nothing."

"Good thing I've got a badge to show anyone who pulls me over. A badge is a get-out-of-jail-free card."

"Slow down and be safe. I'd feel terrible if you get into an accident because of me, and there's nothing you can do right now anyway."

"Nothing I can do?" he said. His tone changed from anxious to flirtatious. "I was hoping that, at the very least, I could take your mind off things."

"How do you propose doing that?"

"I could tell you," he said, "but I'd rather show you."

His words had my breasts sitting up in my bra and taking notice. "Promises, promises."

He chuckled. "I don't know what's going on exactly, but there's one thing I'm sure of. You need to resign from the Pawn and Pistols audit. *Pronto.*"

"But I'm nearly done," I argued. "And the work was going to bring me a nice fee."

"Would you rather have the income or your life?"

"My life, of course," I said. "But the least you could do is let me bitch a little about all the unpaid work Arielle and I have done."

"Bitch away," he said, "but resign that audit immediately."

"I will," I said, "as soon as the cops here let me go."

"You wearing those earrings I got you?"

"Of course."

"Good."

A few minutes later, I'd answered all the questions posed by the officers on the scene, and loaded my office valuables into my car. In a small town like T-Weed, we didn't have specialized crime scene teams, so the officers who'd responded also photographed the scene and gathered the spent bullet casings that littered the street, using tweezers to pick them up and dropping them into plastic bags.

I didn't want to leave Buddha in the car or take him into the pawn shop, so I swung by Daniel's place and left my cat in the converted garage. I gave him a kiss on the head and booped his tiny pink nose. "I'll be back soon. Miss me while I'm gone, okay?" His responding purr told me that he would.

I drove to Tumbleweed Pawn & Pistols. Their marquee sign out front announced tomorrow's sale. SATURDAY ONLY! 20% OFF ALL GUNS AND AMMO! All of the Stockton men drove pickups, and the four trucks were parked side by side in the lot. One was white. One was silver. One was midnight blue. And the final truck was black.

I parked next to the last truck and climbed out of my car. As I made my way to the front door, I ran a hand over the hoods of the trucks. All were cool, and there were no tell-tale *plink* sounds of an engine cooling. This fact didn't entirely reassure me, though. Enough time had passed between the shooting and now for the motor to have cooled off.

I entered to see that the whole family was working on the shop floor. Sharon. Warren. Remi. Chester. Ruger. The boys were polishing the guns, while Warren was once again replenishing the ammunition inventory. Sharon cleaned the floor with a theater-style sweeper.

I passed the display of assorted used tablets and cell phones. Some of the items I'd seen there before had sold and been replaced with other secondhand devices, including an inexpensive flip phone that appeared to have hardly been used. As before, all were plugged into a power strip so that they'd remain charged at all times.

Sharon looked up. I greeted her with a "Hello," and nodded to the men. "Hey, guys."

Warren shook his head. "Heard what just happened at your place. Heard there was a couple other places shot up last night, too."

News traveled fast in a small town like Tumbleweed. Of course, in the case of the shooting at my office, the news only had to travel across the square.

Sharon put a hand to her chest. "It's crazy! What is this world coming to?" She rested her palm on the end of the sweeper handle and cocked her head. "You okay, Debbie?"

"I'm fine," I said. "I'm sure it was just some bored frat boys shooting things up on a dare." Not for a second did I think the shooter had been a student, but I figured it was best to play it off. "You know how those college kids can be."

"Well, I'm glad you weren't hurt." She raised her brows in what appeared to be a hopeful gesture. "Please say you've come by to say you've finally confirmed things with Big D Gun Depot. I'd love to get this durn audit behind us."

"I'm so sorry, Sharon," I said, "but I have to resign from the audit."

Her mouth fell open. "You do? Why?"

"I've discovered I have a conflict of interest with another client. I didn't realize it until I'd already dug into things. I know this will put y'all behind, and I apologize for that. But at least my resignation won't require your new CPA to make a disclosure to the bank. It shouldn't jeopardize your ability to get the loan." *Not like firing me would have.*

She exhaled a soft huff of air. "I suppose that's a good thing, but it's a shame you can't finish. Thanks for letting us know."

"I'll return the retainer you've already paid me." I gestured to the marquee through the window. "Good luck with the sale. I hope you make a killing."

"Me, too."

I turned and headed to the door. My feet slowed of their own accord as I approached the display of used cell phones, and my eyes locked in on the like-new flip phone. When I realized the Stocktons were all looking my way, I forced a smile and continued out the door. I stopped just outside it, though, and pulled my cell phone from my pocket. I scrolled through a few images of Buddha until I found the pic I'd taken of my office landline's caller-ID screen, the one that showed the phone number for the man who'd claimed to be from Big D Gun Depot, the alleged Gordon Mingus.

I committed the number to memory, then switched over to my keypad to dial the number. I put the phone to my ear. Just as I heard it ring through the earpiece, I heard the tell-tale ring of the flip phone inside. My heart performed back flips in my chest. *Holy shit.* If I'd doubted whether the Stocktons were involved in shady gun deals before, I had no doubt about it now.

I doubted it even less when the door opened and Ruger grabbed me, yanking me back inside and throwing me to the floor before I could gather my wits and run. The Stocktons descended on me like a trained team of Navy SEALS, yanking my phone from my hand and moving me around. I flailed and kicked to no avail. Five on one wasn't exactly a fair fight.

Warren pulled my purse from my shoulder and handed it to his wife. "We've got to ditch this."

Sharon took my purse. "She got one of them smart watches? Take it off if she does."

Ruger grabbed my wrist to take a look. "No."

Ruger zip-tied my wrists and ankles while Warren slapped a piece of duct tape over my mouth. Remi turned the sign on the pawn shop's door to CLOSED, while Chester rushed around, closing the blinds on the windows so nobody could see inside. They dragged me into the storeroom and opened the backdoor. Sharon had pulled up her car close and had the trunk open.

No. No, no, no!

Ruger and Remi picked me up and tossed me into her trunk. I wished I'd had a chance to eat my lunch from Golden Dragon first. It would have made a nice last meal and made me heavier to lift. I landed with a *thud* in the trunk. They tossed a big shovel in after me, and the edge of the metal blade hit me in the forehead. *Ow!* I screamed "You mother-fucking assholes!" at the top of my lungs, but with the duct tape in place the curses sounded like nothing more than mere muffled nonsense. A trickle of blood wound its way down my forehead to my brow, and my heart pounded so hard and fast I thought I might have a heart attack.

The trunk slammed closed—*Bam!*—and I found myself trapped in total darkness. My head went light as the engine started and the car began to move. I'd always heard that, if possible, you should never let a kidnapper take you to a second location. Whatever the creep planned to do, it would be much worse in a remote, isolated location of his choosing rather than in the place where he—or in this case *they*—abducted you. But there was nothing I could have done in this situation, no chance I could have beat them or escaped.

Panic gripped me. Tumbleweed was a small town, and it wouldn't take long to reach the city limits. Beyond that, we were surrounded on all sides by a wide expanse of desert. If the Stocktons got me out to the desert, I'd be doomed. I forced myself to take slow deep, breaths in an attempt to calm my mind and think. *What can I do now?* My best hope was to kick out a taillight or get the trunk opened, but with my hands tied behind me I couldn't reach for the trunk release. It was pitch black in the trunk, not a lick of light anywhere. For the next minute or so, I kicked my feet against the top of the trunk and tried to make as much noise as possible, hoping someone would hear me as the car drove by and summon law enforcement to check things out.

When kicking proved ineffective, I wriggled to the back of the trunk and rubbed my shoulder hard against my cheek, trying to dislodge the duct tape. I tried over and over and over until finally the end loosened. A few seconds later, the tape had peeled back far enough that part of my mouth was exposed. I opened my mouth as wide as I could and wriggled my lips, using my tongue to push against the tape and loosen it further.

I raised my head in the pitch blackness and used my bruised forehead to feel for the trunk release. Moving my head along the center top of the trunk, I felt nothing, nothing, nothing, until the cool, smooth edge of a plastic handle against my hairline. *That's it!* Raising my face, I used my teeth to grab the handle. I pulled my head back with all the force I could muster and the trunk popped open. *Pop!*

The sudden sunshine was like a spotlight in my face. I blinked to clear my eyes and caught a glimpse of the big Texas sky above, blue and bright, not a cloud in it. A dust cloud was being kicked up around the car though. *We must be in the desert.*

I tried to sit up, hoping I could somehow throw myself over the side of the trunk without killing myself and the Stocktons noticing me escape. But it was no use. They must have seen the trunk come open, or an indicator light on the dash. The driver floored the gas pedal and the force brought the trunk lid down again before I could stop it.

I hollered at the top of my lungs. "Fuuuuck!" A futile effort, most likely, but at least I'd outwitted the damn duct tape and could hear myself scream.

I tried to use my mouth again on the trunk release, but had less luck this time. The driver had gotten wise to me, and weaved back and forth, keeping me and the shovel sliding around hopelessly in the trunk. *Fuckhead.* The Stocktons were lucky I wasn't prone to motion sickness or I'd have filled their trunk with vomit.

A few minutes later, the car slowed to a stop and the engine was turned off. The car doors slammed shut and foot-steps sounded around the trunk. The trunk popped open again and, before my eyes could even adjust to the light, the three Stockton boys had pulled me from the trunk.

I wrangled and wriggled in their arms, but it was no use.

They attempted to set me on my feet. I glared and curse and went wet noodle on them, refusing to support myself. I dropped to my ass in the sand, raising my own little dust cloud. My eyes and nose filled with dirt particles, and I sneezed. *A-choo!*

Ruger backhanded me across the face. *Smack!* "Stand up, bitch!"

"Fuck you!" I screamed. Tears of rage and terror cleared the dust from my eyes, and my gaze scanned across the family. "Fuck you, and you, and you, and you, too! Fuck you all, fuckity fucking fuckers!" My insults were likely a futile gesture but, if nothing else, cursing at them made me feel better. I might not be able to fight them physically, but I wouldn't go down without assaulting them verbally. "You stupid shit-for-brains idiots!" That curse was hopelessly redundant, but eloquence hardly mattered at this point. "You ugly turd faces!" Seriously, I needed to up my insult game. As a CPA, I had little practice intentionally offending others.

Sharon Stockton slapped me this time. "Shut your mouth! Don't you talk to my boys like that!"

I glanced around. For miles, all that was visible was the empty blue sky, the open desert, and prickly pear cactus topped with its bright pink fruit. *I'm fucked.*

Warren retrieved the shovel from the open trunk and handed it to Ruger. "Dig."

I watched in horror as Ruger began to dig what had to be my grave. We were in the middle of nowhere. *Would anyone even find me out here?* It would be hard enough for Hayleigh to lose her mother, but if I disappeared without a trace it would be even worse. And Buddha! What would happen to my fat, lazy cat?

After a couple of minutes of digging, Ruger wiped sweat from his brow and held the shovel out to Chester. "Your turn, bro."

Chester took over. I flung my legs, trying to kick sand and

dirt back into the hole. Ruger grabbed me under the arms and pulled me back. I tried to roll away, and they didn't even try to stop me. There was no need. In any direction I went, my progress was stopped by the sharp needles of prickly pear. Lest I turn myself into an unwitting porcupine, I decided the best thing I could do was conserve whatever energy I had left to fight them when they tried to toss me in the grave.

Dust continued to blow into all of our faces as Chester handed the shovel to Remi. "You're up."

But wait. Is that dust in the distance behind the Stocktons? *It is!* The vehicle was too far off for me to get a good look, and it was possible it wasn't even headed in this direction. But in the off chance someone was coming to my rescue, I figured the best thing I could do was distract the Stocktons.

"Hey!" I hollered. "The least you can do if you're going to kill me is tell me what's going on."

Sharon chuckled. "I suppose there's no harm in that." She turned to her husband and sons. They all shrugged. Having received their implicit approval to proceed, she turned back to me. "We've been buying stolen guns from a guy who operates under the name Big D. We don't even know the guy's real name. Chester met him at a gun show in Fort Worth years ago. That part of what I told you was true. Big D got your phone messages and got nervous. He warned us that we'd better get you off his ass, so Ruger called your office from a burner phone he'd bought in Dallas, pretending to be from Big D Gun Depot. He got the name Gordon Mingus from two of the towns he'd passed when he drove to Dallas to buy the phone."

The burner phone was the one that had shown up on my caller ID with the 214 area code, the number I'd called earlier that rang in their shop. They'd either been too stupid to hide the evidence or too greedy to forego a buck or two from reselling the phone. "Was Ruger also the one who called my office and warned me to resign from the audit?" That caller's number had come up as unknown on my caller-ID.

"No," Sharon said. "That call came from Big D himself. It was a couple of his cohorts who broke into your apartment. Big D directed them to kill you. When that plan went south, they did the drive-by at your office. They'd have kept trying if you hadn't come to our shop to resign from the audit today and forced our hand. But when that burner phone rang, we knew you'd caught us. There was no way we could pretend to have been mere dupes."

"Big D has guys to do his dirty work for him? Does that mean it's a big operation?"

"Huge. The operation spans across the southwest. I've heard he sells guns to the drug cartels south of the border, too. He's got a guy who works as a metal fabricator for an industrial outfit. The fabricator files off the serial numbers and puts on new ones so that the guns look legit. He does such a good job, they fool everyone. We've had local cops, even ATF officers come by our store to do random checks. None have batted an eye." She chuckled, gloating that they'd fooled law enforcement.

Warren chimed in now. "That new Tumbleweed cop wasn't any wiser. He bought a stolen pistol from us yesterday, as a matter of fact. He ran the number through the National Crime Information Center system right in front of us to make sure it was good. It cleared. He even thanked us for giving him such a good deal. Our law enforcement discount."

At that, the entire Stockton family shared a good laugh.

It was the last laugh they'd share for a good, long while.

CHAPTER 11
A BANG-UP JOB

THE DUST cloud in the distance grew closer, and I could see flashing lights atop the vehicles now. *Thank God!* Ruger, Chester, and Remi picked me up once again. Also, once again, I didn't let them move me willingly. I wriggled and kicked, and whipped my head back to smash Ruger in the nose. *Crunch!*

"Fuck!" My shoulder fell to the ground as he dropped me to grab his nose. Blood streamed between his fingertips. He wobbled on his feet for a second or two, then his eyes rolled back in his head and he collapsed to the ground in a dusty heap.

"Ha!" I cried. "What a wimp! Scared of his own blood!"

Sharon fell to her knees next to her prone son. Warren, on the other hand, wore a look of disgust on his face. He toed Ruger's butt with the toe of his cowboy boot. "Get up, son. It's just a little blood. Nothing to lose your shit over."

While their parents tended to their brother, Remi and Chester shifted so that one held each end of me now. Chester was at my head, careful to keep his face back far enough that he wouldn't suffer the same fate as his brother. The two carried me over to the long, deep hole and swung me back and forth, gaining momentum with each swing.

"One!" Remi called as I swung to the left. "Two!" he called as I swung back to the right. Three!"

With that, they released me. I soared for a second before plummeting into the hole. *THUMP!* I landed hard on sharp rocks and loose, sandy dirt. The force of the impact knocked the wind out of me, and I fought to catch my breath.

Tossing me into the hole was a big mistake for them. With me now safely out of the line of fire, the approaching law enforcement could take aim. All I could see from inside my grave was the sky above and a trio of circling buzzards, who were probably hoping to have me for a late lunch. But I could hear the sudden *woo-woo-woo* of sirens now, and the *pop-pop-pop* of bullets hitting the ground and cactus around the area above me. I could also hear the thuds and curses as the Stocktons dove to the ground. Seconds later, the *chop-chop-chop* of a police helicopter entered the mix.

As I stared up at the sky, a storm of bullets whizzed over me. The Stocktons shot back. *Bang-bang-bang!*

Pop! Bang! Pop-pop! Bang-bang-bang!

From above, Sharon shrieked and cried, "I'm hit!"

Warren hollered, "Stand down, boys! Put down your guns and put your hands up!"

They're surrendering! Thank God! Relief surged through me.

I waited in my grave, the sirens growing louder as law enforcement approached. I heard the sound of vehicles sliding to a quick halt on the sandy soil nearby, followed by doors opening and pounding feet. Dust and pebbles fell into my hole, and then a face appeared above. *Daniel.* Though it was his day off, he was dressed in his uniform. He'd probably worn it to Fort Worth to make sure the guys at the ATF took him seriously.

I looked up at him, shaken yet relieved. "What do you say we polish off that bourbon tonight?"

"Thank God you're okay!" He bent over, putting his hands on his knees and closing his eyes for a moment as if in thankful prayer.

"How did you find me?"

He grinned. "Those god-awful earrings you're wearing? They've got GPS chips embedded in them. They're actually intended for dog collars, but I was able to attach them to wires I took off another pair of earrings."

"Clever. I'd just thought you had terrible taste in jewelry." Thank goodness he'd had the foresight to fit me with a locator device.

He eased himself down into the hole with me. He whipped a pocketknife from the front pocket of his pants and cut through the zip ties. I rubbed my wrists and ankles. He gingerly pushed back my bangs to inspect the cut on my forehead. "We'd better get that looked at."

While another officer reached down to take my hand, Daniel formed a stirrup with his palms. I stepped into it and he hoisted me up. I stepped onto firm ground to see a dozen law enforcement officers on site, both Tumbleweed police and county sheriff deputies alike. The Stocktons sat lined up on the ground, their hands shackled, their faces scowling. Chester and Warren both had prickly pear tines sticking out of their faces. They must have dived into a cactus when they'd taken cover. *Ha!*

I sent a smile Sharon's way. "By the way, I've changed my mind about that retainer. I'll be keeping it after all."

———

Over the next few weeks, the ATF lab confirmed that dozens of the guns in the Tumbleweed Pawn & Pistols inventory were stolen with fake new serial numbers.

The Stocktons, once a close-knit family, turned on each other, each of them blaming the others and claiming they were innocent in the deal. Eventually, and on his attorney's advice, Chester broke, agreeing to give information on the stolen-gun supplier in return for leniency. The information he provided led to a dozen arrests of major players in the illegal gun trade, including Big D himself.

Daniel—*Officer Mooney*—was commended publicly by the police chief and mayor for his part in the investigation. Hope McIntyre did a nice write-up about him in both the newspaper's print and online versions. She did a story on me, as well, entitled "Numbers Don't Lie."

Buddha and I moved into our new house, and found it to be a wonderful home. It was comfortable and easy to maintain. My cat enjoyed watching the birds outside the bedroom window.

My practice got so many new clients that I had to move to bigger digs and hire another CPA to keep up. Seemed everyone wanted to hire the hero CPA who'd played a part in bringing down a dangerous gun ring in Tumbleweed.

As for Daniel and me, well, we finished off that bottle of bourbon. I'm not one to kiss and tell, so let's just say we'd also found ourselves to be completely compatible in all regards. For the time being, I'm enjoying my new home and my new independence, and I'm enjoying this new romantic relationship, as well. Like a tumbleweed, I don't know where the winds of life will take me now, but I'm looking forward to finding out.

THE END

ENJOY THE ENTIRE SERIES!

Enjoy the entire Trouble in Tumbleweed series!

Four authors. Four stories. One Town. And a whole lot of trouble ...

This small west Texas town might sit in the remote desert, but it can't hide from trouble. Someone's always trying to kill someone else for one darn reason or another, and things get as tangled and twisted as a tumbleweed. The Trouble in Tumbleweed series is an entertaining and interrelated collection of mystery novellas from some of the genre's most popular and bestselling authors including Melissa Bourbon, Christie Craig, Diane Kelly, and Lawrence Kelter.

More about the other books in the series:

MELISSA BOURBON – THE TROUBLE WITH HOPE AND GLORY

Hope and Glory McIntyre are about as different as sisters can be. Glory is the quintessential Texas beauty queen, while Hope wants nothing more than to dismantle Tumbleweed's beauty queen scene with the mighty stroke of her journalist pen. Glory's dreams of becoming Mrs. Tumbleweed might be over when her rival is found dead, and while they might be as different as water and Texas oil, Hope won't rest until she clears sister of wrongdoing and gets to the truth.

For more about Melissa and her books, visit her website at www.MelissaBourbon.com.

CHRISTIE CRAIG – THE TROUBLE WITH EXES

Everything happens for a reason, but sometimes that reason is that you're daft and make dumb decisions.

When it comes to men, Cassie McGee is a champion at picking losers. Hence, Cassie is in Tumbleweed, Texas, hiding from an abusive ex-husband. Life gets hairy when an ex-boyfriend, now a private detective, learns Cassie is in danger. He and his flatulent, dishonorably-discharged K-9 show up to play knight in shining armor. Ahh, but Cassie's done being a damsel in distress.

On the scumbag Richter scale, Pierce Jacobs doesn't compare to Cassie's ex-husband, but his mistake sure managed to hurt her. When it becomes clear someone in Tumbleweed is conspiring with her scoundrel ex-husband, Pierce is determined to smoke out the culprit. Between setting smoke bombs, dodging bullets, and investigating wacky Tumbleweeders, can he keep them alive long enough to convince Cassie he deserves a second chance?

For more about Christie and her books, visit her website at www.Christie-Craig.com.

LAWRENCE KELTER – THE TROUBLE WITH THE TUMBLEWEED TWISTER:

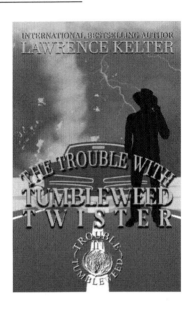

Tough times have put the squeeze on auto mechanic Smoky Rolle. Forced with losing his home, Smoky accepts an easy money side job from his cousin Travis. What should've been a quick fix goes sideways when Travis is abducted at gunpoint leaving Smoky to wonder if Tumbleweed is the sleepy little West Texas town he believed it to be or if something nefarious is bubbling beneath the surface. Secrets lead to lies and lies to larceny in this pulse-pounding smalltown mystery.

For more about Lawrence and his books, visit his website at www.LawrenceKelter.com.

NOTE TO READER

Enjoy Diane's Other Books and Series!

Dear Reader,

I hope you enjoyed this story as much as I enjoyed writing it for you!

What did you think of this book? Posting reviews online are a great way to share your thoughts with fellow readers and help each other find stories best suited to your individual tastes.

Be the first to hear about upcoming releases, special discounts, and subscriber-only perks by signing up for my newsletter at my website, www.DianeKelly.com.

Find me on my Author Diane Kelly page on Facebook or at @DianeKellyBooks on Twitter and Instagram.

I love to chat with book clubs! Contact me via my website if you'd like to arrange a virtual visit with your group.

See below for a list of my other books, and visit my website for fun excerpts.

Happy reading! See you in the next story.

Diane

BOOKS BY DIANE KELLY

Above the Paw

The Long Paw of the Law

Paw of the Jungle

Bending the Paw

The Tara Holloway Death & Taxes series:

Death, Taxes, and a French Manicure

Death, Taxes, and a Skinny No-Whip Latte

Death, Taxes, and Extra-Hold Hairspray

Death, Taxes, and a Sequined Clutch (a bonus novella)

Death, Taxes, and Peach Sangria

Death, Taxes, and Hot Pink Leg Warmers

Death, Taxes, and Green Tea Ice Cream

Death, Taxes, and Mistletoe Mayhem (a bonus novella)

Death, Taxes, and Silver Spurs

Death, Taxes, and Cheap Sunglasses

Death, Taxes, and a Chocolate Cannoli

Death, Taxes, and a Satin Garter

Death, Taxes, and Sweet Potato Fries

Death, Taxes, and Pecan Pie (a bonus novella)

Death, Taxes, and a Shotgun Wedding

Other Mysteries and Romances:

The Trouble With Digging Too Deep

Love Unleashed

Love, Luck, & Little Green Men

One Magical Night

A Sappy Love Story

Made in the USA
Las Vegas, NV
30 August 2022

54367022R00059